Forget Me Not

Claudette Hubert

ISBN: 9781736604007 (Paperback)

Any references to historical events, real people, or real places are used fictitiously. Names, characters, and places are products of the author's imagination.

Front cover image by Devin Flood
Book design by Devin Flood
Foreword: Mark Leach
About the Author: Sheri Hansen
Editor: Colleen Brightman

Printed by Amazon in the United States of America.

First printing edition 2021

Graves Publishing
44 Spring St.
Fairhaven, MA 02719

Instagram: @cjh_author_creator

Dedicated to Jocelyn and Charlotte: May this book be a constant reminder that hard work and perseverance is what makes dreams come true.

Foreword

I have the privilege and honor to write the foreword for the book you are about to read. The author is Claudette Hubert. She is a first-time author and I am lucky enough to be her friend. The entire world has just experienced one of the strangest times in its history and has completely changed everything in our lives.

Because of our new daily work circumstances, I was able to witness the entire process of Claudette's journey to write this book. It was fascinating, intimidating, occasionally frustrating but ultimately was an incredible experience for me. Writing words isn't one of my skills, so watching someone with a natural gift such as writing or any other creative endeavor, work through their process is so fascinating to me. Watching someone write thousands of words a day, seemingly without effort, is so impressive. I am certainly not suggesting this pursuit was not without a Herculean effort, but to this observer Claudette made it seem that way. I suppose that's the real gift of someone's talent. Making something so incredibly difficult look so easy.

The other part of this journey that is important to acknowledge is that this is not Claudette's job. This is her dream. Since the 3rd grade, she knew then she had this talent and because of the crazy circumstances of the past year, she started her trip to fulfill this dream.

Now that you have some of the back story, read the book. You will enjoy it. You will be entertained and you will be surprised. But what I really want to say is when you have the chance to impact someone's life in a positive way, do it. The best part of any friendship is watching your friend's dream come true right in front of your eyes. I am so proud of this achievement and even more proud of Claudette for overcoming all the obstacles put in her way along her journey. Having friends like Claudette makes life better. And who knows, maybe you'll be the inspiration for a character in a book or better yet be asked to write the foreword.

Prologue

The pain was unbearable. She bent over trying not to fall down. She gripped the edge of the railing so hard her knuckles were white and her nails actually left imprints on the palm of her hand. It was a miracle they didn't draw blood, she was gripping so tightly. Her hand was the least of her problems right now. Her back felt like it was literally on fire. It felt as if someone was standing behind her with a blow torch just heating her up from the inside out. All day she felt upbeat. It was the first day she felt like having this baby wasn't an enormous mistake. She had struggled with the idea of having a baby at such a young age. She was still a baby herself. She agonized with the choices before her once she acknowledged the test was actually positive and she wasn't hallucinating. Keeping the baby wasn't a decision she came to lightly. She actually sat down and made a list of the pros and cons. There were far more words on the con side, so many that she found herself having to flip the page to list them all. On the pro side were two words. "Precious and love." Those two words tipped the scale for her. How could she willing give away her own flesh and blood? Abortion wasn't an option. She was raised to believe that abortion equaled murder and she couldn't bear the idea of being a murderer.

She could feel another contraction coming on. Her doctor told her that once labor started her body would know what to do. Her body may know, but she was scared as hell that she was going to split in half. Everyone told her labor wasn't that bad. It's all worth it in the end. She tried to squat down on the steps hoping the pain would subside.

"How can women endure hours of this intensity?" she asked herself as she tried to catch her breath.

She didn't attend any child birth classes for several reasons. One, she didn't have a coach. Her mother had thrown her out when she finally broke down and told her she was pregnant. She was literally on her own, but not for long. Ready or not this baby was going to be making an appearance. Bethany wasn't ready. She dreamed of the moment when she would be able to hold her baby but wasn't prepared for her current situation. Two, she couldn't afford the classes. She was living in a rooming house and barely making ends meet. The elderly lady who took care of the house felt sorry for her and told her she could move in and would give her a break on the rent, provided she could help out with the household chores. Bethany would have done anything to ensure a roof over her head. Any little money she was able to make early on in her pregnancy was used to buy second hand clothes and diapers. She knew it wasn't going to be easy but she was still immature and believed that love would prevail over any obstacle.

By the time Bethany dragged herself into the hospital she felt like she could collapse at any minute. Her face was as red as a cherry Jolly Rancher and she could barely breathe. The walk took her over an hour since she had to stop several times whenever a contraction came on. She lived two blocks away and foolishly never anticipated this amount of pain. She had heard women say labor was 'uncomfortable'. To her, that was the understatement of the year, that was like saying habaneros only have a slight kick to them. Thankfully a nurse saw her walk in and immediately yelled for an orderly to get Bethany in a wheelchair.

As they raced down the corridor, Bethany felt a gush between her legs. She assumed her water broke and was relieved. She knew when the water broke the baby wasn't far behind. The orderly took the final corner to her room on what felt like two wheels of the wheel chair. If she weren't in so much pain, she may have even enjoyed the ride, but right now all she wanted to do was lie down and say a prayer that everything would be alright. She couldn't wait to meet her baby.

The orderly adjusted the brakes on the wheelchair and leaned over to help Bethany up out of the chair. "I think my water broke. I felt something burst a few minutes ago." She said, clenching onto his arms for dear life.

The orderly, with the name tag, Adam, flexed his muscles to help relieve the pressure of her grip. "Don't worry about it, the nurse is on her way in to take your vitals and she will check you out. For now, let's just get you into bed." Adam replied looking down at the dark stain in between her thighs and traveling down her pant leg.

Instantly Adam knew there was a problem. He had worked in labor and delivery long enough to know blood when he saw it. He gently laid Bethany in bed and told her to stay calm and just keep breathing. He tried not to run out of the room, not wanting to worry her but he needed to get to the nurse's station STAT.

"Hi Bethany, my name is Mona and I will be your nurse until midnight. Let's take a look and see how far along you are shall we?" Mona had been a nurse for many years and took her job very seriously. She loved what she did and had a talent for making expectant mothers feel a little more at ease at the most painful time in their lives. "How long have you been having contractions dear?" Mona asked as she wrapped the blood pressure cuff around Bethany's arm.

"They started about eleven this morning. I thought my back was just sore from leaning over, or what I consider leaning over with this", she said as she rubbed her enormous belly. "I was folding all the baby's clothes and putting them in the dresser. It was when I stood up straight that I felt a sharp pain. My belly got hard as a rock and I thought my knees were going to give out from under me." Bethany admitted a little embarrassed.

"Yup, that's a contraction for sure. No need to worry you are here now and we are going to take good care of you. By this time tomorrow you will be holding your little one in your arms and will have forgotten all about this pain." Mona said making a note of her blood pressure. It was higher than Mona would have liked but her patient was very young and no doubt scared out of her mind. She made a mental note to check it again after Bethany got settled in, hopefully it will be a little lower. Her temperature was elevated. Mona wasn't all that concerned. Her patient could be dehydrated, perhaps the fever would subside once she started the IV fluids. As the nurse moved the blankets down to the bottom of the bed, she noticed it. Blood. A lot of blood. This wasn't good. She immediately used the phone to call for a team to come in and assess the situation. She wasn't a doctor and didn't want to panic, that would only cause her patient to get more agitated. Some blood loss during delivery is normal but this amount this early in labor was cause for alarm.

Two more nurses and the doctor rushed into the room. The doctor was putting on a gown and gloves while one of the nurses hooked Bethany up to a fetal heart monitor. The other nurse was administering the IV set up in Bethany's right hand. Mona squirted gel onto her patient's belly. Bethany thought all this commotion was normal for someone in labor. Her being so young and naïve was actually a good thing at the moment. She wasn't as emotional as some other mothers Mona has seen. The gel was so cold it caused Bethany to wince. She was familiar with this portion of this procedure. She knew in only a few moments she would see her baby on the screen in front of Mona. Mona slid the transducer probe across Bethany's belly. She could hear the heart beat but sadly it wasn't as strong as she had hoped but then she saw something. At first, she wasn't sure she was seeing it clearly. Could it be just a shadow picked up by the machine? Was it really there? Mona took a closer look and tried to contain the expression on her face.

"Doctor, I think you need to take a look at this." Mona said with trepidation in her voice. "I think we are dealing with a multiple birth here and one of them is in distress." Mona said as she turned the screen so the doctor could have a clear view of what she was looking at. Mona was a veteran nurse in labor and delivery. With over twenty years at this hospital and on this ward alone, she knew damn well what she was looking at, her name tag may say R.N. and not M.D. but she was certain this poor girl may lose both her babies. The doctor leaned over and took a quick glance at the ultrasound monitor.

"We need to get her to the O.R. right away", still leaning over with his hand between her legs. One of them is coming within minutes and its breech. If the placenta has ruptured I would rather have her on the table than delivering naturally. I don't want her bleeding out, so let's go, move it!" the doctor yelled.

All the nurses flew into action with military precision. One was putting an oxygen mask on Bethany who by now knew she and her baby, or as it turned out, babies were in serious trouble. She closed her eyes causing tears to stream down her face. Could this really be happening? Could she lose her baby? Was there really more than one? So much was running through her mind she tuned out the immense pain she was in. She couldn't think. She wasn't prepared to make sense of everything she heard. She knew this was happening, she just couldn't accept that it was actually happening to her. She wished her mother was here with her, to keep her calm and tell her everything was going to be ok.

The nurse told her to lay on her side, something about getting more oxygen to the baby. She could barely hear her, there was so much noise around her. She had her eyes closed for most of the trip to the operating room. She was chanting prayers over and over in her head, it was almost like she was trying to cast a spell. Anytime she did open her eyes she was able to see all the women in their various rooms holding their babies, even though the gurney was moving at a pretty good pace. Some of the rooms whipped by in a blur but what she couldn't see she could certainly hear. Babies crying. She closed her eyes even tighter, begging God, begging anyone, to allow her to hear her baby cry. She wanted nothing more than to be a mother. She knew it would be the hardest work she would ever know but she created this life, she felt it move every day, it was a part of her. She couldn't bear the thought of the baby being taken away before they had a chance to meet.

It was literally minutes from the time she saw the O.R. doors open to when she turned her head and saw this gigantic pink blanket surrounded by the tiniest little face Bethany had ever seen. She couldn't believe it. She was staring at her daughter, only minutes old, but there she was, pink and shiny. Brand new to the entire world. Until this very moment Bethany wasn't aware how much love one person could feel. This was a love like no other, something she never felt until this very moment, something she never wanted to ever live without.

Bethany wasn't even sure how it happened. She was being transferred from the gurney to the operating table and a nurse noticed the baby's bum was out and the rest of her precious daughter was quick to follow. She remembered the doctor telling her a natural delivery wasn't in her best interest but mother nature had a different plan, because in the blink of an eye her baby was born perfectly healthy weighing six pounds two ounces. In the next blink she was staring at her daughter and then she remembered nothing. She was out. When she awoke, the nurse was sitting in a chair holding her baby. As she stirred in the bed trying her best to shake the groggy feeling from her head, the nurse made a call and immediately her doctor and priest, following close behind, walked into her room.

"Bethany, I am Dr. Pimental, how are you feeling?" he asked.

She shrugged her shoulders not able to bring herself to speak. She wasn't in as much pain as she was when she first arrived at the hospital but she was definitely uncomfortable. She felt like someone had taken a soldering iron to her belly. She glanced over to the nurse holding her baby. Why isn't she bringing her to me, she thought.

"I have brought along Father Martinez, because I have some difficult news to tell you," the doctor continued.

Bethany was terrified as to what was going to come out of the doctor's mouth. All she could think was that someone had determined that she is unfit to take care of her baby, a daughter she hasn't even had a chance to name yet. "I can take care of my baby. I may be young but she is all I have in this world, please don't take her from me." She pleaded with tears in her eyes.

"Miss Mitchell is it? I am not here to take your baby from you. I am sure you are going to make a fantastic mother. What I came here to tell you is going to be difficult but it has nothing to do with the beautiful bundle sitting over there with Nurse Hansen. Last night when you came into the hospital you were in active labor. The tests and procedures that were performed caused us some serious concern. The ultrasound showed more than one fetus. Baby A, which we refer to as the one Nurse Hansen is holding is in excellent health. Though she was born in an Occiput Posterior position everything went well. Unfortunately, Baby B was born with various complications. She has compromised lungs and can't breathe on her own. We can't tell for certain why any woman goes into labor when she does and we aren't sure what caused Baby

A to develop in utero to full term and Baby B did not. Baby B is in the NICU and we have a machine breathing for her. At this point, it is your decision if you want to continue with these measures." I know this is a lot to take in which is why I have Father Martinez here with me. There is a notation in your file that you are Catholic, so I wanted you to have someone you could speak with in case there are any moral dilemmas with making your decision."

Bethany didn't say a word. She was speechless. She couldn't even begin to think of anything to say. How was she supposed to react to news of this magnitude? The only thing that she could think about right now was the tiny infant in the nurse's arms sitting in the chair across from her.

"Nurse, will you give her the baby please?" Father Martinez nodded his head for the nurse to get up. As the nurse stood Bethany couldn't help but extend her arms out waiting for her baby to join her in the bed.

"Here you go mommy, she is going to start to fuss in about an hour, if you would like to try breast feeding someone can come in and show you how to do it." The nurse said with a sweet smile as she placed the baby in her mother's arms. Bethany has never heard herself referred to as mommy. It was a term she didn't think she would ever get tired of hearing. She looked down at her precious gift from God and couldn't imagine she was destined for anything other than loving this baby with everything she had.

"Bethany, she certainly is a beautiful child. Have you thought about a name for her yet?" Father asked holding his rosary in his left hand making the sign of the cross with his right. He placed a hand on the baby's head and quietly said a small prayer for the child.

"I haven't really had a chance to think about anything yet. Yesterday I felt her in my belly and now here she is. Here they both are. This all happened so quickly it doesn't seem real. I have twins. Two daughters. Father, what am I going to do? How am I supposed to do this? Is it wrong for me to keep her hooked up to machines that are breathing for her? Do I decide to just let her go?

Isn't that a sin? Oh Father, you have to help me. I don't know what to do here. I don't know how to make this kind of a choice." She cried. She pleaded with the priest to help her make the right decision.

It took every ounce of strength she had, she knew in her heart she would never be able to care for two infants, never mind one that was sickly. Even if Baby B survived, she wouldn't be able to take care of her. The doctors didn't think that the baby would live much longer than a few minutes once the machines were turned off. She didn't know how she would ever be able to forgive herself but she decided that turning off the machines was the right thing to do. In the end if the baby was to live, she would. She had filled out all the forms for Baby B to be placed for adoption in the event she was able to beat the odds and survive. If the machines were really all that was keeping her alive, she knew deep down in her core that no human being should live that way. Bethany finished signing all the appropriate forms and was wheeled into the NICU. She wanted to be there when they turned off the machines. The last thing she wanted was for her precious daughter to die alone. There was very little noise in the NICU. Mainly sounds of machines helping tiny humans fight for their lives. When she approached her daughter's incubator, the tears just started streaming down her face. "If only I had known you too were in my belly, I would have tried harder, prayed harder, or drank more milk. I would have done anything for you to be healthy like your sister. I am so sorry this has happened to you. Please be at peace my love, knowing every minute I will be thinking about you until we meet again. See you later alligator." She mumbled all this to herself, her voice so quiet, her face so close to the incubator. The childhood phrase about the alligator was something her mother always said to her when she left for school each morning.

"We are going to turn off the machines now." The doctor told her.

She thought she would have been strong enough to sit there and watch her little girl float off to heaven but she couldn't bear to watch her drift away. She told the nurse she wanted to go back to her room and grab her things. She held her baby, the precious little girl whom she named Fiona, as tightly as she could. She wanted to leave the hospital as quickly as possible. She would never forget her other daughter but she wasn't capable of dealing with the guilt that was consuming her. She felt like she was abandoning someone who needed her just as much as Fiona. Just as the nurse turned the corner out of the NICU she heard the faintest little cry. A baby's cry. It wasn't more than a whisper but a mother always knows the sound of her baby's cry......

One

The moonlight showed through the curtain panels of her bedroom just enough for her to catch a glimpse of the raindrops illuminating her window. It had stopped raining hours ago but the last of the raindrops were as stubborn as she was. They would slide down the window in their own time. Fiona laid in her bed staring out the window mentally willing herself to fall asleep. Sleep was a foreign subject to her these days. Since the accident happened, she wasn't able to get back to a normal sleep pattern. There were nights when she fell asleep as soon as her head hit the pillow only to be wide awake two hours later. Other nights she tossed and turned searching for a comfortable spot in bed and out of nowhere she was out like a light waking up after the sun rose feeling more refreshed than she had in weeks. Those nights were few and far between but she was grateful when they did happen. If not for those nights she wasn't sure she would manage to function in a coherent state. Her therapist tried to prescribe her medication to aid in the sleep department but Fiona was dead set against it. Doctors these days were much too eager to prescribe a miracle pill. It seems there was a pill for everything. Again, stubborn. She knew the only way to get the rest she desperately needed was to turn off her brain. The pattering of the rain soothed her back to sleep but the nightmare began all over again.

She closed her eyes but she couldn't shake that night from her memory. It was tattooed on her brain, an invisible scar she would carry around for the rest of her life. Detective Arthur Lever wasn't just a partner, he was her mentor, a father figure, and an all-around beautiful human being. Technically she knew the accident wasn't her fault but in her heart she felt responsible. She closed her eyes trying to clear her mind but it was no use, that dreadful night floated through her mind like a trailer for a movie.

It was a freezing bitter cold night. The wind gusts were causing power outages throughout the entire state. The hail was coming down so hard it actually stung when it hit your skin. Arthur and Fiona were settling in for the night on a stake out. Arthur was prepared as he always was. He had his thermos of coffee, sandwiches in case he got hungry and a blanket. He was a seasoned vet when it came to stake outs. Fiona on the other hand, this was her first. She didn't think to pack anything other than her gloves, phone and gun.

"You have to be practical when planning a stake out Mitchell. It's not like you see on television. Tactical operations like these could take days not just a ten-minute segment before the television show goes to a commercial break. Stake outs are a commitment and need to be executed properly." Arthur explained to her. He handed her a blanket. He knew she wouldn't think to bring anything but the police issued necessities so he made sure to bring along some extras for her. "Next time you are on your own. I am not sharing. You should be grateful I took pity on your sorry ass tonight." Arthur scolded her in a friendly manner. They were very close, having bonded over murders and drug dealers, not to mention Fiona grew up without a father. She never knew how much she longed for a strong male figure in her life until she had met him.

"If you could just close the window a bit I wouldn't be sitting here freezing to death." Fiona quipped back at him. There was a severe age gap between the two of them but the banter they shared seemed like they were old friends.

"If I shut the window it will get warm in here, warmth will cause us to get sleepy. If we fall asleep, we are no longer on a stake out, we are just two idiots who fell asleep in a car." Arthur replied adjusting the collar on his jacket to cover his exposed neck and ears.

Silence filled the car, the street was dark, it didn't seem like tonight was going to be the night they caught the drug cartel they were investigating. The pair had been working this case for months. Their C.I. had given them a tip a shipment of heroin was coming in from Mexico and was supposed to be delivered to the house across the street. This wasn't the first time they attempted to catch the dealer in the act. This guy was slippery, somehow always managing to get away.

Just before two a.m. Fiona looked down the street. Her binoculars didn't show anything but darkness. The night was pitch black it was impossible to see your hand in front of your face. This would be the perfect night to move the kilos of heroin. Fiona saw what looked to be a puff of smoke. It's wasn't a cigarette. She didn't see the glow of the bright orange tip. This was a person, walking down the street. They must have been dressed in black because the only thing she could make out was the smoke. She smacked Arthur in the shoulder rousing him out of his sleep. They took turns sleeping in two hour shifts only to be awoken if something definite was happening. She had woken him up twice for no apparent reason but this time, this time she was certain she had something.

"Mitchell, I swear to God if you wake me up one more time to ask me if I am warm enough, I am going to take out my taser and practice my distance shooting using you as the dummy." Arthur grumbled pulling his blanket up under his neck.

"Boss, listen, I think I see something this time. Seriously, you need to wake up." Fiona said pulling the blanket off him causing the winter air to slap him in the face. He sat up in the driver's seat, blinking a few times trying to shake the sleep from his eyes.

"What have you got Mitchell." He said taking the binoculars from her.

"See that puff of smoke down the street. It's getting closer, I think that's a person. I think that's our guy. He is all dressed in black, wanting to blend in with the darkness of the night but he didn't plan for it to be so cold. His breath is giving him away. It's like his own personal GPS tracking device." Fiona explained pointing down the street but the darkness made it impossible to see her hand gestures.

"Good eye, let's see where his breath takes us." The two followed the breath for ten minutes as he slowly made his way up the street to the front door of the dealer's house. "Call the team up the street and let them know to get into position." Arthur instructed her. There was a beat up dark blue van parked a few houses up with several S.W.A.T. team officers just waiting for the ok to storm the house.

Fiona did an initial sweep of the front lawn and then the back. There were only two entrances and a bulk head door leading to the basement. The S.W.A.T. took position flanking the back yard. Fiona and Arthur were pressed flat against each side of the front door. The wind was howling, the rain was picking up. There wasn't much cover on the porch, both partners were wet and freezing. Fiona could feel her heart beating in her ears. This was it. There was no turning back now. As Arthur gave the signal to the lead agent to use the battering ram to breach the door Fiona saw it. A glowing red dot just below

Arthur's neck. She tried to yell for Arthur to move but the commotion from the battering ram made it impossible for him to hear her. Just as the door came down, she heard the gun shot. Fiona jolted awake, covered in sweat. She was panicked and breathing heavy. Her doctor said the nightmares would go away in time. It had been over a year, wasn't it time for them to go away?

Two

Fiona Mitchell stood tall at five foot two inches, not exactly the average height for a woman in her early thirties, but what she lacked in the height department, she more than made up for in more womanly areas. She was stylish yet always tried to dress comfortably. In her line of work, she never knew where she would end up from one day to another. Her long red hair was consistently pulled back away from her face when she was working. In the evenings or during social engagements her long red hair with its natural curl could certainly turn a head or two. Her hair wasn't her only head turning feature. Fiona developed early in the chest area, a feature that made her self-conscience during her teenage years but she had learned to ignore the stares and mumbled comments, most of them being made by girls in her school more so than boys.

"Every girl your age is dealing with the same issues Fiona. Some develop early while other girls think they will be flat chested their entire lives. You need to keep that in mind when girls say things about you. Everyone has insecurities, making comments isn't polite but girls your age are struggling the same way you are trying to come into their own," her mother often said to her. She had a small frame, not weak but by any means but not overly muscular either. She was strong enough to be confident she could handle herself in most physical situations.

It was social events she was now struggling with. What happened to Arthur made it difficult for her to be able to carry on a conversation without going into a full-blown anxiety attack. She was petrified someone would ask her for details on what really happened that night. She felt nauseous just thinking about it. It was a tragedy. Why couldn't people leave it at that and just let her get on with her life? People were curious by nature. It's in their blood. She still heard the whispers and comments as she walked through the halls, feeling like high school all over again. She knew she was never going to be respected since losing her partner was still fresh in everyone's mind. The infamous woman who watched her partner get shot in front of her. Helpless to do anything to save him. She has been referred to as a victim, a murderer, and a liar. The department finally cleared her of any wrong doing but in her heart she knew it was her fault. Learning to live with that fact has been harder than she anticipated. Nothing prepares you for a loss like that. In the academy you are trained to watch your partner's back. She didn't, she failed him. Not technically because of her, but if she was on her game, he would be here now. The first thing anyone asks when an officer is shot in the line of duty is "Where was their partner?"

These are the times she missed her mother the most. Some days she was lucid and Fiona didn't want to bog her down with sorrowful tales that she wouldn't remember the next day. When her mother, Bethany, was having what the nursing home called a good day she wanted to enjoy it with her, not complain about the job regardless of how hard it was on her lately. Early onset dementia has robbed them of the time they thought they would always have together. Fiona always imagined she would watch her mother grow old but still be fully independent just at a much slower pace. Little did she realize at the age of thirty-three would she be putting her fifty-year-old mother into a nursing home.

Fiona didn't come to the decision lightly. At first her mother was having very few bad days. She would be forgetful about random things, what time a T.V. show was on or which channel, getting phone calls wishing her a happy birthday that was months away or even forgetting to turn the lights off at night. Fiona took all these little quirks in stride thinking it was cute that her mom was flighty. It wasn't until she left the car running all day, in the driveway with the front door wide open during a snow storm, that she knew her being flighty was an understatement. Thankfully one of the neighbors called Fiona, who was able to rush over. If she were on a case, she wouldn't be able to get away and tend to her mom. This was a thought that became a major concern for Fiona. She walked up to the house and at the foot of the front steps she looked straight into the living room and saw her mother watching a soap opera in Spanish. Between the two of them many a swear word have been said, some in other languages but never have either of them ever been able to understand a conversation in Spanish.

It was clear to Fiona that her mother needed more care and attention than she could provide given her unpredictable work schedule. She moved back into the small house she grew up in to be with her mom as much as she could. Fiona hired the woman across the street to check in on her a few times a day and into the evenings whenever she was called out because of the job. Mrs. Appleton was more than willing to help out. She had lost her husband a few short months ago and needed something to keep her occupied. Mrs. Appleton and Bethany got along very well. They would watch t.v. together and play cards. Many times, when Fiona called throughout the day to check in on her mom they were bickering back and forth over a game of pitch. Fiona would always be eternally grateful for Mrs. Appleton. If it weren't for her, she wouldn't have been able to keep her mother home as long as she did. Sadly, the day had come leaving Fiona no choice but to put her in a home. She tried to convince herself it was for her mom's own safety but it isn't easy for any child to see their parent failing, unable to help them. When Mrs. Appleton called and said that she couldn't convince her mother to come back in the house after taking her shower she knew something had to be done. She found her mother walking up and down their street totally naked in the middle of November. In New England November was a funny month, it could be a bitter cold or a spring like day. Either way, Bethany wasn't in her right mind and something needed to be done. This wasn't something that could be categorized as flighty. Most of the neighbors were aware of Bethany's illness but it didn't make it any less embarrassing for her mother or the neighborhood.

Fiona consulted with her doctor and together they decided that her mom would be safer in a more secure establishment. Bethany was all that she had left in life. Her father was a no show for most of her younger years and now she didn't feel the need to have a relationship with him. If he didn't want me then why should he want me now, was her theory. Last she heard he was living somewhere in Canada. He sent a Christmas and birthday card every year to her mother's house addressed to Fiona. She never sent anything back to him. She couldn't bring herself to forgive him for abandoning her and her mother when they needed him the most. As far as Fiona could remember it was always just her and her mom. Being an only child had its perks but it's times like this she wished she had a sibling to share some of the burden with.

Three

The phone on the nightstand rang startling Fiona. Only one of two people could be calling. The home giving her an update on her mother's condition or the department telling her she caught a case. She wasn't sure which she wanted more. "Detective Mitchell" she said in to the phone trying not to sound nervous, even though she was.

"Hey Mitchell, its Vargas. A body was found this morning and you drew the short straw." Vargas and Fiona went as far back as the academy. They came up together and became fast friends. They both worked the foot beat when they first joined the force. After a few years, Fiona wanted to sit for the detective exam but Vargas was perfectly happy staying on as an officer. He encouraged her to climb the ranks. Vargas and his family were a second family to her. She was always invited to any celebration that was being held at the Vargas residence. She was given a standing invitation to join them for dinner, though she rarely attended. Jeannie, Varga's wife, and Fiona became good friends as well. She was the first to call after Arthur was shot. Even though Jeannie was only the wife of a cop, she knew Fiona well enough to know she needed all the Vargas family support and not just her husband Reggie's. "It takes a village to raise a child and to be a cop's wife," she used to say to Fiona.

"What do we know?" Fiona asked throwing the down comforter off of her bare legs, feeling the cold morning air hit her skin caused shivers down her spine, or so she hoped, this was no time for her nerves to get the best of her. She needed to be on her A game.

"All I know is she washed up on shore and was found this morning by a homeless man, that's all I got." Vargas replied.

"Alright then, tell them I will be there within the hour."

She disconnected the call and rushed to the bathroom. After a cold shower, to ensure she was fully awake she threw on a pair of black jeans, a department issued t-shirt and her police issued windbreaker. The weather was brisk for this time of year but she knew when she got excited, she started to sweat. She didn't want to give any of the boys in blue a reason to think she couldn't handle the pressure of a new case. She was working with a new partner, this being their first official case together. This was her first time being the lead detective on a case. Fiona hadn't had a chance to meet her new partner yet. She knew the pairing was only short term until a permanent partner could be assigned to him. All she knew was he was the son of some politician and was fast tracked into the homicide division. Fiona was determined to make a good impression all the way around. She wrapped her holster onto her left shoulder, removed her gun from its case, slid it into the smooth leather, took a deep breath and walked out the front door.

Four

The wind was whipping violently the closer she approached the ocean. With every step she could feel the bitter cold against her exposed skin. The sky was overcast yet clouds were still visible. Fiona hoped the weatherman was wrong in his prediction of rain this morning. Rain wasn't good when investigating a homicide. There wasn't going to be much evidence if the body floated up to shore, perhaps there would be some evidence on land that could help her get a starting point in her investigation. Ocean water would have washed away all traces of DNA. Already Fiona felt like she was fighting a losing battle.

Yellow crime scene tape spread across the entire length of the beach. The stone wall was used as a barrier against the prying eyes of innocent bystanders also known as neighborhood busybodies in addition to the intrusive press. Today, they arrived on scene before she did. Could it be this wasn't the type of case that can be solved which is why they assigned her to it? Is it because she wasn't qualified for a "real" case? Usually, detectives try to pawn off a water case because the closure rate on those types of murders wasn't very high. Fiona realized she was becoming paranoid. This was her case and she was going to work it no matter what little evidence she was able to gather. Whoever the victim was, they had a family, parents, and maybe even children. Someone must be looking for them. All she was confident about was there was a body and she needed to find out who it was. It hadn't yet been confirmed if it was a homicide or simply an accidental drowning. From what Vargas told her when he called it in didn't necessarily mean death with foul play.

"What have we got?" Fiona said to Su Lee Ming, the medical examiner. She squatted down next to the body, needing to pull her head up like she was looking at the sky. Instantly her eyes started to water. The stench was palpable. A dead body carries its own scent, but one that washes up on shore has the stench of the ocean mixed with it. It was an odor unlike any other. She thought back to her former partner, hearing his voice in her head. "Once you experience it you will never be able to forget it. Always make sure you are carrying a jar of menthol in your pocket. Believe me it will come in handy." Oh how she wished he were here with her right now. He had a knack for keeping her calm whenever she let her nerves get the best of her.

"Female, approximately twenty-two to twenty-five years of age. Cause of death looks to be strangulation." The M.E. used her pen to point to the ligature marks around the victim's throat. Fiona noticed the cavity of the eye sockets, blackened and shriveled like rotten tomatoes. The sockets were sunk into her face having no eyes left to hold them open. Various fish and sea creatures had feasted on this woman. Her face was unrecognizable. It simply didn't look human.

"Wow, someone really did a number on her." Fiona said to Su Lee.

"Whatever wasn't done by the killer, was done by whatever lives deep in those waters." Su Lee replied using the same pen to point to the ocean behind her. "I'll know more once I get her on the table and open her up." Su Lee loved a good mystery. She knew the cause of death but the way she looked at Fiona, she knew there was more to this than just strangulation.

"What aren't you telling me Su?" Fiona asked in a low tone. Her and Su Lee hadn't worked together that often since she became a detective but her reputation was well known around the squad room. "This is my chance to change what people think of me. I don't want any surprises." Fiona stood up trying to get the blood to rush back to her feet. Squatting on sand was much harder than it looked.

"Listen, I know you got a bad rap last year. Whatever I know, you will know. I will keep you posted after I open her up but the ligature mark tells me she didn't drown; she was dead long before that. The question is, was she killed here or just dumped?" She winked at Fiona as she walked back to her team.

Officer Adams walked up to Fiona with a homeless man trailing just a few steps behind. "Mitchell, this is Davis, the man who found the body." Fiona nodded her head as a salutation because shaking this man's hand was not in the cards.

"Davis, nice to meet you. Can you tell me what you were doing out here at this time of the morning?" she asked taking her notepad from the inside of her coat pocket. Fiona glanced at her watch, it was barely six a.m.

"I was making my rounds. I make rounds every day."

"What do you do on these rounds?"

"I look for loose change, empty cans. I redeem them at the liquor store across the street. Sometimes I get lucky on Mondays and can get me a bottle before noon. Kids like to have parties here on the weekends. Never do clean up after themselves. One time I found a half-eaten pizza. That was a good day." Davis replied proud of his find.

"You found a lot more than soda cans today Davis. Can you tell me about that?"

"I was walking down the beach when I saw something a ways down. I thought it was a pile of seaweed. Sometimes if there were kids here late at night, they leave their cans and garbage in the seaweed pile. I ran over thinking I hit the jackpot. Was really lookin forward to getting me some hooch this morning. It's a bit cold out here this time of year." Davis responded wiping his mouth with his filthy finger less glove. It wasn't the kind of finger less glove all the teenagers were wearing. His glove had so many holes his actual fingers were sticking out. If it weren't for the fact that the glove was blue and his fingers were covered in dirt, she wouldn't have noticed the holes.

"I am sorry you weren't able to get the prize you were looking for but can you tell me about the girl? Did you touch her, move her or anything like that? Were there other people around? Did you see anyone on the beach when you found her?"

"I didn't do nothing. I walked up to the pile, saw that it wasn't seaweed and there were no cans. I leaned in and saw that it sort of looked like a gal. I crossed the street, and had the guy at the store behind the counter call youze guys. I ain't in trouble, am I? I didn't do nothin!" Davis was visibly nervous and getting worse by the minute.

"Davis, listen to me. You didn't do anything wrong. You did the right thing by getting someone to call us. I just need to make sure that no one messed with the victim after you found her. If you touched her, I need to know. I need to exclude you as a suspect. Am I going to find your DNA on her?" Fiona tried to sound as soothing as possible. She wanted to reach out and touch his shoulder so Davis could be reassured he wasn't in any trouble but she couldn't bring herself to lay a hand on him. He had a stench that was so pungent she thought it was permeating into her clothing. The dead body smell was something she was used to but this foul odor was more than she could tolerate.

"I told you I didn't do nothing. Is there a reward in this for me? I did find her ya know?" Davis was getting more agitated by the minute.

"Let's go over to the store across the street. I will talk to the cashier and then we can see about getting you a reward. How about some breakfast?" Fiona asked extending her arm out to show Davis what direction they were walking towards.

"I like my breakfast in a glass made by Mr. Johnny Walker himself." Davis replied walking ahead of Fiona, wanting to show her the way. Fiona wasn't sure if standing in front of him or behind him was going to help the odor that was dripping off him. It was barely time for people to get up and get ready to start their day and already she had a dead woman with no I.D. and all she could think about was getting into a hot shower and scrubbing the sour scent away.

Davis sat on the bench next to the bus stop slowly sipping his nip. The store clerk gave it to him after hearing he wasn't hallucinating about finding a body. Fiona walked out of the store writing in her notebook, not watching where she was going. A bicyclist rode by her so close it knocked the notebook right out of her hands.

"Watch it!" the bicyclist shouted. Fiona looked in the direction of the two wheeled offender and could only make out the sleek point at the back of the rider's helmet and sneakers. Bright green with orange and no laces. True blooded cyclists always had flashy gear. It helped motorist see them from a farther distance. She never understood the sport. She rode her bike as a child but it was more a means to get from point A to point B, and certainly not for pure enjoyment. Once she got her driver's license, she never touched her bike again. Her mother on the other hand rode her bike all over town every Sunday.

It was her idea of exercise. Now, Bethany couldn't even balance on a stationary bike in the athletic room at the nursing home.

"You need to watch where you are going Detective. The people around here could care less who is in their way. Last week I almost got hit by a hog leaving the bar on Second St. The guy was cool, he pulled over to make sure I was okay. We went back to the bar and he bought me a couple rounds."

"Yeah, I need to watch where I am walking." She replied. "Thanks for all your help this morning Davis. Do you remember what I said to you when I gave you your reward?" Fiona wanted to make sure there was no confusion.

"Yeah, I ain't no dummy. I gonna wait here with Officer Adams until the cruiser pulls up. No lights since I ain't in no trouble. I go with the officer to the station. I tell him everything I told you and then I write it down and sign my name. I got it. I don't need no one tellin' me things twice." Davis said looking annoyed that Fiona interrupted his drinking time.

"Understood Davis" Fiona said saluting him. "No more Mr. Walker until you are done at the station. The money I gave you can be spent after that. The officer will bring you back here and you can do what you like at that point." Fiona looked into his eyes, wanting to make sure he understood what she was saying. Many times, homeless people suffer from various mental health issues. It's not always easy to communicate with them and know they fully understand you. Most haven't been on their meds in years, some have never been on meds. It's sad to see but there isn't much that can be done for them. Davis seemed like he had all his marbles rolling in the same direction which was a blessing considering he was a key witness in the discovery of the body. It is doubtful he would ever have to enter a courtroom but if so, a hot shower and new suit would be her biggest worry and not the mental status of Davis Foncesca. Fiona was determined she wasn't going to let anything jeopardize her case.

After sending Davis on his way with a patrolman she walked back over to the stone wall making her way past the crowds of onlookers and the press.

"Detective, was this a drowning or was foul play involved?" one reporter asked shoving a microphone in her face.

Fiona looked at the reporter and said, "No comments at this time. We will let the public know when the notification has been made and there is something accurate to report." Fiona pushed herself through the crowd making her way back to the damp sand.

"Detective Mitchell?" a man asked walking up to her. He was dressed in a pair of jeans and a blue blazer. He resembled a modern day extra from Miami Vice. "I just told the mob of reporters over there that I have no comment. I am going to have to ask you to stay on the other side of the wall behind the yellow tape. This is a crime scene I won't have you contaminating evidence." Fiona said barely looking up.

"I'm sorry, I am not a reporter. I believe I am your new partner. The name is Julian Correira." The gentleman extended an arm for a handshake.

"My apologies. It's been a bit of a hectic morning." Fiona replied shaking the man's hand admiring his manicured nails. She looked up at him and saw a chiseled chin, dreamy blue eyes and a full head of sun kissed blonde hair. There was no way this man was a local. This was not the time for Fiona to find someone handsome, let alone have to work so closely with. She needed to keep her head in the game. She was given a case, a murder case. This was her time to shine. A time to make up for the wrong she had done. This was a chance to prove to the department and herself she was born to be a detective.

"It's a pleasure to meet you. Have you had a chance to get any info on the case?" she inquired. Fiona assumed she was to be the lead detective. She had been with the force for a few years and he looked as if he just flew in from a movie set. It was almost like he was too good looking to be a cop.

"Yes ma'am I have. Looks like the swimmer washed ashore sometime in the early hours. The coroner mentioned she didn't have much to go on until the autopsy was done. Said she would be in touch with you once she knew more. I take it it's too soon to see what she has determined." Julian said looking around to see if he was still in her line of sight. Fiona walked a few feet from him but was able to still hear what he was saying. Something in the sand caught her eye. Julian walked over to where she was standing and looked down. He too noticed it.

"Is that a diamond ring? With blood on it?" he asked.

"That Detective Correira, is exactly what it is." Fiona stated waving over the C.S.I. team. "Make sure you get a picture of this and bag it as evidence."

"Seems like our lady was engaged or married. Can't imagine someone would want to leave a rock like that lying around on the beach." Julian made a notation in his notepad and put it back in the inside pocket of his sports jacket.

"I agree, even if a woman were to lose her ring that doesn't explain the blood. No woman is going to cut her hand and not notice her ring is gone. Woman notice things like that all the time. They get used to the weight of the ring on their finger." Fiona explained.

"Unless of course the blood wasn't from her hand. If she was cut on some other part of her body then she may not have noticed the ring was missing, especially if she was in a struggle with someone. She could have been more concerned about the amount of blood she was losing. What if the ring was ripped off her finger by an attacker?" Julian spoke aloud, he found it helped him sort things out in his head.

"You sir, are thinking like a detective." Fiona said, impressed with how he asked questions like a seasoned veteran. "Have you been in town long? Have you had a chance to get to know the area?" Fiona asked again walking ahead of him thinking perhaps this wouldn't be the worst partnership.

"I was born and raised in this small town. Got sick of seeing the same faces day after day so I decided to attend college in Florida. Being the son of the Governor has its advantages growing up but it also came with its own set of disadvantages." Julian explained to Fiona.

"Wait, you're telling me your father is Governor Manuel Correira?" Fiona said hearing the shock in her own voice.

"The one and only." Julian replied arrogantly. Fiona could feel her pulse start to quicken. This was the last thing she needed. She was paranoid enough trying to gain back the respect she lost after what happened last year only to be partnered with the son of the most powerful and influential Governor this state has ever seen.

Five

Fiona started the car barely waiting for her new partner to shut his door. "What's the rush?" Julian asked trying to get his seat belt fastened.

"I noticed a marking on the inside of the ring, I think I may know the jeweler who designed it."

"Hmm, definitely must be a woman thing. Men wouldn't think to look for a trademark." Julian mentioned marking something in his notepad. "I have a habit of writing down odd tid bits I learn on the job. I figure it may come in handy in future cases." Julian said a little embarrassed that Fiona saw him taking notes like a high school student.

"Whatever you need to do to remember the facts. It's the little things that are often over looked and usually the one thing that will crack a case wide open," Fiona instructed him as she pulled into a no parking zone. Julian gave her a look and then looked over at the parking ban sign. "Perk of the job," she said as she exited her vehicle.

They both crossed the street, the moment they got under the awning of the jewelry store it started to rain. Heavy rain. Both Fiona and Julian looked at each other, knowing whatever evidence they didn't collect at the crime scene was now long gone. This wasn't going to be an easy case. Not only was she breaking in a new partner, and trying to re-establish a name for herself with her peers, she was faced with a homicide that had very little evidence. She had the deck stacked against her, but she has faced harder battles than this. Never alone, Arthur was always by her side but this time she was going to have to face this one on her own. Her cell phone dinged. She glanced at it wiping rain drops from her forehead. The rain was really coming down. The text was from the medical examiner requesting to meet her at the coroner's office but gave no other details. This day just keeps getting better and better. Here she was trying to follow up on the ring and Su Lee needed her for some reason. This better be good she said to herself.

Julian got to the car before she did and grabbed some tissues from the glove box. "Here, do the best you can," he said as he handed her the crumpled bunch.

"This weather is pissing me off. Of all days for Mother Nature to get a hair across her ass," she replied. He would learn soon enough that she was the type of woman who meant what she said and said what she meant. There was no in between with her. You never had to guess where you stood with Fiona. She made it crystal clear if you were on her shit list.

"I know, we have lost whatever evidence we may have had after she washed up on shore. This isn't how I pictured my first homicide case." Julian remarked looking at her while she pulled out of the spot without even checking her mirror. He was overly cautious and she was more reckless. He chalked it up to letting her nerves get the best of her now that she was back on the force after the mandatory leave for anyone being apart of an officer involved shooting.

He knew all about his new partner and what happened last year. It wasn't a secret but he didn't want to push. He wanted her to trust him and that took time. He knew she would open up to him at some point. He could wait. He would keep an eye on her but at the same time he was willing to let her set the pace on how quickly she wanted to reveal the details regarding the hardest day of her life. Maybe when this case was over, she would trust him well enough to let him in.

They arrived at the M.E.'s office fifteen minutes later and were both soaked from head to toe by the time they pushed through the double doors labeled Morgue, authorized personnel only. She should have checked in with security but she knew her way around this place only too well. There were many times she and Arthur paced this hallway waiting on the results of an autopsy. Arthur taught her everything she knew about being a detective and it was her duty to keep that tradition alive.

"This better be good. I had a lead I was following up on and had to rush over here in traffic with what feels like a tsunami out there." Fiona was in a mood. She didn't like people derailing her from her train of thought. She wanted to talk to the jeweler. She had a gut feeling he could give her some insight on the ring they found on the beach. Granted it could wait but it still put her in a sour mood. Being wet didn't help either.

"Girl, you are going to love this. You wouldn't have believed me if I told you over the phone that's why I had you come down here. I knew you would want to see it for yourself." Su Lee explained sensing Fiona's mood not wanting to delay the unveiling any longer. "Voila" she said as she placed an evidence bag into the palm of her hand.

"Are you kidding me? Where did this come from?" Fiona asked with a small smirk on her face. Things like this fascinated her. She loved when she heard about strange things happening in the morgue. Both Fiona and Su Lee enjoyed any odd occurrence in the morgue. "This is from my body?" Fiona asked unable to take her eyes off the little bag placed in the palm of her hand.

"The very one. I noticed the Digitus Mi'nimus Ma'nus was missing and instantly thought it was from some form of sea life." Su Lee started to explain to Fiona but noticed Julian was looking confused. "Digitus Mi'nimus Ma'nus is the Latin word for the pinky finger," she said directing her raised eyebrow directly in Julian's direction. "Some fish will eat almost anything. It wasn't until I got her on the table and started my initial physical examination that I noticed I couldn't open her mouth. It was sewn shut. Literally sewn with a needle and blue thread. After I unstitched her lips, I found something lodged in her throat. I thought I was living out the morgue scene from Silence of the Lambs but there it was. No leaves or seaweed, just the Digitus Mi'nimus Ma'nus nestled neatly between the victim's adenoids and tonsils."

"Are you telling me this was in her throat? Bag and all?" Julian asked looking a little green. It wouldn't be the first time someone vomited in her morgue but she had a rule. You puke, you clean. She was fine with dead bodies and their fluids but she was squeamish around any bodily fluids from a living human.

"Julian, maybe you should step into the hall, you don't look so good," Fiona said not even taking her eyes off the bag. She had been in Julian's shoes before and just from the tone of his voice she could tell he was about to be sick.

"Here, chew on these." Su Lee said handing him a couple Altiods. "The peppermint is so strong not only does it settle the stomach it actually makes the odor a little easier to bear," the M.E. informed the rookie detective giving him a quick wink.

Julian was handsome, there was no avoiding that. His chiseled good looks made it hard to tell he was a detective. Most rookies lose their lunch on their first trip to the morgue. Fiona made a mental note to give him shit about it later. Even though she knew exactly how he felt, and had literally been in the same position only a few short years ago, she couldn't let him think she was a pushover. Fiona wondered if his good looks were going to be a problem. She wasn't one to mix business with pleasure but he was eye candy for sure. She pushed those thoughts out of her mind to focus on the matter at hand. She silently chuckled to herself. Severed finger, matter at hand. There were moments when she acted like a child. She could admit it, she was just glad she kept those child-like jokes in her head and didn't let them out of her mouth. She was a professional and needed to act like one, especially when breaking in a new partner.

"So, we know she had a finger bagged and lodged in her throat. What else do we know?" Fiona asked needing as much information as the medical examiner could provide. She didn't really have much to go on considering the entire crime scene has been washed away between high tide and the downpour that was still raging outside. Fiona had to admit, other than the fact that the storm killed anything that could help her in solving this case, the sound of the raindrops pelting off the window was rather soothing. Maybe her therapist was right. Maybe she should give those sounds of nature CD's a try at night when trying to sleep.

"Your victim was in relatively good health considering she was a heavy smoker. Her lungs were toast, damage is far too advanced for someone her age. She may have been on the vape kick everyone was on a few months back." Su Lee wasn't one to judge anyone's lifestyle but she could never understand why anyone would want to ingest poison in their body. "It's sad really, she was a beautiful girl. Whoever did this, knew what they were doing. No way did she drown. She was strangled. I would bet good money it was with some sort of nylon rope. Whoever took her life was at least a good four inches taller than her, based on the angle of the ligature marks on her neck," Su Lee mentioned as she walked to the other side of the metal slab. "See here, the markings are showing in an upward pattern aiming higher at the back of her neck at the base of her hairline." Su Lee ran her finger across the ligature pattern on the victim.

"That doesn't necessarily mean the killer was taller. The Vic could have been sitting in a chair and the killer came up behind her." Julian chimed in with a tone of satisfaction in his voice. He knew he was right. He knew there were many scenarios to explain how she was strangled.

Su Lee gave him her evil stare. She didn't care for him contradicting her in her own lab. She was reporting her findings. He was the detective. His job was to prove who actually did the deed, out there in the world. In her office she was the boss. "Good Luck with this one," she said to Fiona just as Julian pushed the swinging doors to the morgue open. "He looks like he is going to be one insufferable prick," she said as Fiona held her hand out making sure the swinging door didn't hit her in the face on her way out.

"So much for chivalry Julian." She mumbled under her breath. She would find a way for her partner to pay for his rudeness later.

Six

Fiona and Julian pulled up to the jewelers, again. Julian looked at his watch and then Fiona. He wasn't going to say anything. His partner certainly seemed like she was in a foul mood. Sr. Flannigan was just about to turn the open sign to closed when both detectives approached the door.

"Well well, if it isn't Fiona Mitchell in the flesh. I haven't seen you in ages." Sr. Flannigan had been retired for years, handing the business over to his one and only son, but from time to time he liked to come into the store and make sure things were running smoothly. It wasn't for lack of confidence in his son, it was more of something to do to keep his mind sharp, and stay out of the house so as not bother his patient wife.

They had both taken over the shop when Sr. Flannigan's father retired. The shop had been in business since 1910. It has been one of the longest running businesses in the state. After his wife had their third child, Mrs. Flannigan decided it was best to be a stay-at-home mom. They spent very little time together as a couple from that point on. He was always working and she was home with the children and then as they got older, carting them from one sporting event and dance rehearsal to another. By the time all the children were asleep both parents were so tired themselves they could barely keep their eyes open. Now that all the children had grown and moved out of the family home, neither husband or wife knew what to do with both of them being home at the same time.

"What brings you in Fiona? Are you and this handsome gentleman here looking for a diamond ring by chance? It would make your mother so happy to see you settled down. How is she?," the store owner asked, always making a point to remember all his customers and their loved ones. Love is the main reason the store has been able to stay in business as long as it has. As long as people are in love, there will always be a need for good jewelers.

"Um, no. We aren't together. We are only partners. I mean, we aren't partners like a couple, we are both detectives. He's my detective partner." She replied knowing she was turning various shades of red. She had a knack for making herself look stupid from time to time.

"Oh, I see, so tell me are you here in an official police capacity?" the old man mentioned, leaning against the door, raising his eyebrows in curiosity. He was always interested in any local gossip. Helps with business, he used to say.

"Actually, we are. I was wondering if you could tell me who purchased this ring?" Fiona asked fishing the evidence bag from her pocket. The inside pocket was still damp from this morning's downpour. Thankfully the ring was sealed in the bag. Whatever evidence could be detected was safe inside.

"This is definitely one of our pieces. This was custom made by my son. He always adds a distinct marking on the inside of all of his pieces. He is paranoid about people trying to copy his designs," Sr. Flannigan said while rolling his eyes. "If memory serves, I believe this piece was paid for in cash. Wait here, I will check the records."

"If this piece was custom made, it shouldn't be hard to track down not only who bought it but for who," Fiona mentioned while looking in the glass case she was leaning against. She thought about what it would feel like to love someone so deeply to want to spend the rest of your life with that person. She was turning into a cynic at such a young age. She never believed in love. The idea of being that vulnerable to another person was far scarier than anything she had ever experienced, on or off the force. There were some chances even she wasn't willing to take.

"Hello, anyone in there?" Julian said waving his hand in front of her face. She blinked a few times when he caught her attention. "Where were you just now? You looked like you were deep in thought." Julian asked.

"Sorry, I was just thinking about something. I wish Senior would hurry up. If we can get a name from him, we will have a place to start looking in order to identify our victim. I don't want her being referred to as Jane Doe. No one deserves that," she said as she leaned over the jewelry counter trying to see if the old man was coming back with any pertinent information.

"You are in luck. Thankfully the one thing my son learned from me is how to keep meticulous records. "Let's see" he said skimming the page in a book that looked to be almost as old as her partner. "Ah yes, here it is. This piece was purchased back in 2017. It was made based on the customer's specifications. He gave my son the liberty of designing it anyway he wanted as long it had at least ten karats and was made in all platinum. He spared no expense this guy. It was one of the most elaborate pieces we have ever done. My son insisted that before he left the shop with it, he have it insured. People these days would do anything to make a quick buck. This piece's final price was just around a quarter of a mil." The man said closing his book.

"I'm sorry did you say a quarter of a million dollars?" Fiona asked, her eyes open wider than the sun.

"Yes, young lady, that's exactly what I said." The shop owner had a prideful tone in his voice. He knew his shop was known for its high-quality work.

"I can't imagine what I would ever do with that kind of money but I can assure you I wouldn't blow it on a ring," she said with a slight attitude. She realized who she was talking to and again felt stupid. She did have a knack for it. "Sorry, you know what I mean. You do beautiful work but this just isn't my thing." She apologized trying to back pedal out of her last comment.

"I understand sweet girl," the owner said taking her hand in both of his. "People these days aren't willing to spend that much either, but some people have money to burn. When it comes to love some people are willing to do anything to show it," the man replied.

"Would you happen to have the gentleman's name that paid for such an extravagant piece of jewelry? We think whomever he had this piece made for may be the woman who washed ashore this morning. We really need to get information about her so we can notify the next of kin, if it's not him of course." Fiona said looking at the old man with pity in her eyes. She has used the 'poor me' look before and it always yielded success.

"My dear, I would be happy to help but I must ask that you keep this as confidential as possible. The man who purchased this ring has a reputation in

this town and I would hate to have anything scandalous linked to my store."
The jeweler replied nervously.

"I assure you; I will use the utmost discretion. There is no reason for
the public to know anything about this ring and who it's connected to." Fiona
reasoned with the man while shaking his hand.

"There are certain things we never release to the press. We keep certain
elements of the investigation and evidence secret so when we apprehend a
suspect, they can tell us things only the actual perpetrator would know. What I
am trying to say is everything you just heard in there, she pointed to the jewelry
store as they drove past it, never actually happened. It doesn't matter who may
ask. Nothing is to be said without my authorization." Fiona looked at him for a
little longer than Julian would have liked. He wished she would keep her eyes
on the road.

"I hear ya loud and clear boss. The fact that this middle-aged man is
getting his rocks off with a girl barely old enough to purchase her own drinks
will never cross these lips." Julian said making a note in his pad and slipping it
back into his jacket pocket.

"We don't know that he was having an affair with her. All we know is
he had the ring custom made and it somehow landed at our crime scene.
Hopefully Mr. Osborne will be able to fill in the blanks, until then mums the
word." Fiona scolded him like a child. This was her case and she wasn't going
to let her partner take part in the rumor mill.

"You're the boss but if you think he wasn't screwing her you are out of
your mind. No man is going to pass up a chance with a woman like that. Even
in the morgue, laying on the cold slab it was obvious she was once a hottie."
Julian teased her, trying to see how far he could push her sense of humor.
Fiona gave him a look, what her old partner called her stink eye. As if on cue
Julian sat up in his seat, looked straight ahead and didn't say another word.

When the detectives arrived at the home of Walter P. Osborne III the
sun was just about to set. There was a chill in the air, a sign that Autumn was in
full swing. The leaves were slowly falling off the trees, bright red, yellow and

orange. In less than a week there wouldn't be a single leaf remaining on any tree limb. That is the one downfall of Autumn, it doesn't seem like a season when it's over in less than two weeks. Before long there would be snow on the ground and sub-zero temperatures. "I hate this part. I hate having to give death notifications, it's one of the worst things about the job. Have you ever had to give one before?," she asked Julian watching him zip up his jacket.

"No, I can't imagine it's something anyone is ever ready for. I am not sure which is worse, giving the news or hearing the news," he said with a somber tone. Clearly, he was no stranger to death. Who is really?

Julian rang the doorbell a second time. The house was gargantuan. There was no other word to describe the monstrosity they were about to enter. He has seen plenty of medieval movies and the castles in those films were a close comparison to this one. "I can now understand what Flannigan was talking about when he said some people just have money to burn." Fiona looked at him with a raised eyebrow. The door opened; Julian couldn't help but notice the sheer width of the door frame. This wasn't a castle; this was a fortress. Whatever this man was into he definitely wanted it protected.

"Can I help you?" a woman looking to be in her late fifties wearing a basic black suit asked. It seemed like she had been crying for some time. Her eyes were bloodshot and her mascara was still puddled under the corner of her eye.

"Good evening Ma'am, I am Detective Mitchell and this is my partner Detective Correira. We are looking for Mr. Osborne, would he be home?," Fiona asked with a gentle tone. Clearly this woman was upset about something but she couldn't just assume it was because of the victim.

"He is in his study. I will get him for you. Please come in, have a seat in the parlor while I get him. Please excuse my appearance I am suffering from a severe sinus infection. Can I get you anything, water, coffee?" she said clearly trying to hold herself together.

"No thank you." Julian responded looking around the expansive room. The walls were decorated with exquisite oil paintings. The floors were vintage hardwood in perfect condition. He assumed people didn't sit in this room very often. Fiona walked around the room toward the wall-to-wall glass window. The view of the backyard was breathtaking, she had never seen grass so green in all her life. There were plenty of people in this neighborhood that were passionate about their landscape, but based on the view she was sure nothing could top this. Julian cleared his throat causing Fiona to glance in his general direction. Her partner was standing in front of the mantel staring at a picture of the victim.

"Fiona, come take a look at this," Julian requested in a whisper not wanting anyone in the house to hear him, or cause an echo due to the cathedral ceilings. "Now why would a man keep a picture of his play thing on the mantel, out in the open for his wife to see?," Julian asked elbowing Fiona in the side.

"The reason the picture is on the mantel is because my wife took that very photograph last month before Felicity went back to college. You see, my wife, Linda is constantly taking pictures. It started out as a hobby and now she is turning down requests for photography jobs. She doesn't want to be forced to take pictures when she isn't in the mood. I am afraid my wife is fickle that way. It's not like we need the money anyhow," Mr. Osborne said spreading his arms out to show off the size of just this one room in the house. Mr. Osborne stood about six foot three, he was insanely handsome even with the salt and pepper grey hair on both his head and goatee. He wore a navy-blue silk shirt and grey cashmere pants. Both of which Julian recognized as costing more than his annual salary. The leather loafers he wore most likely cost more than Julian's car. It was apparent based on his gestures that Walter Osborne thought very highly of himself.

"Mr. Osborne, I am Detective Fiona Mitchell and this is my partner Detective Corriera" she introduced herself extending her hand to shake his. He tipped the crystal tumbler he was holding containing what had to have been hundred-year-old scotch.

"What can I do for you Detectives? I can't possible have that many parking tickets the police would send detectives to my house," he chuckled. Clearly this tumbler wasn't his first of the day.

"No, sir unfortunately I have some rather unsettling news."

Mr. Osborne's eyes widened certainly not expecting any news especially unsettling. "Perhaps I should get my wife," he stated putting the tumbler down on the mantel. Julian silently cringed, that tumbler required a coaster. Julian was a bit of a neat freak. More than a bit, some of his family considered him a little OCD.

"For now, I think it's best we just speak with you if you don't mind. Some of this information is rather sensitive." Julian explained.

"Sensitive? Unsettling? This sounds serious? What exactly are you trying to tell me Detectives?" the high-class gentleman was starting to sober up with each passing word.

"What we need to know is how long have you been having an affair with the woman on the mantel?," Julian said pointing to the picture frame now slightly askew on the mantel.

"I beg your pardon; you can't be serious! That's outrageous! I have never in my life had an affair. How dare you accuse me of such an outlandish thing, and with Felicity no less. She is my pride and joy. How dare you come into my house and accuse me of such indiscretions. Who the hell do you think you are?" Mr. Osborne shouted to the point where he was beginning to sound like the alcohol was about to take over.

"What is all the shouting about in here Walter? Is everything all right?" Mrs. Osborne appeared in the doorway, nervous to move any further into the room without her husband setting her at ease. Mrs. Osborne was obviously familiar with her husband's temper.

"Everything is fine my love, these Detectives were just leaving," her husband replied extending his arm for her to come further into the parlor.

"Sir, I apologize for my partner's rudeness. I assure you I will have words with him later regarding the definition of the words tact and respect but until then I do have some things, I need to discuss with you. You said the woman in this picture her name is, Felicity, is that correct?" Fiona inquired taking out her notepad, her pen at the ready while eyeing the photograph on the mantel.

"Yes, the woman in the picture is Felicity. Why?" Mrs. Osborne asked with a quiver in her voice. Tensions were high and there was a chill in the air all of a sudden.

What is your relation to the woman in the picture?" Fiona questioned the wife. She seemed to be less outraged than her husband at the moment. The detective thought best to give her husband a few minutes to gain his composure.

"Detective, Felicity is our daughter, now will someone please tell us what the hell this is all about?"

"Oh shit," Detective Corriera muttered under his breath. This time it was his turn to feel stupid. Sadly, his stupidity was going to cost him a dressing down as soon as they left this house. He knew it and so did Fiona. No one was going to disrupt her investigation with wild accusations.

"I am terribly sorry to have to tell you this but your daughter's body was found on the beach this morning." Fiona stated trying to be as somber as possible. She didn't have to try very hard at sounding somber. Sadness was the only emotion she seemed familiar with lately.

"Body? Found? Wait, this doesn't make any sense. Are you saying that our Felicity is dead?" Mr. Osborne asked, his face red from either the last of the scotch hitting his blood stream or shock, neither detective was sure of which.

"Yes, I am so sorry to have to tell you this news but I need to know about your daughter's whereabouts for the last twenty-four hours. Anything you can tell us may be of incredible help," Julian stated extending his hand as a peace offering to the now grief-stricken father.

"I am not sure what we can tell you. Last we knew she was going to study with some friends at the library. She called last night just before dinner, she knew I was battling this cold and wanted to see how I was feeling. She said she would be back at the dorm late but wanted to check in before she left," the victim's mother stated between sobs.

"Do you know what time this was? Did she call often?" Fiona pushed, wanting to get as much information as she could before either of them absorbed what had happened and fall apart completely.

"She usually calls two or three times a week. She sends me a text every day with little smiley faces but every now and then she calls just to hear our voices. She wants to be treated like an adult but she still gets homesick. She would never admit it but a mother knows their child." Mrs. Osborne said slowly sitting down in the chair to the left of the mantel. She leaned over resting her elbows on her knees with her head in her hands.

"Mrs. Osborne, are you alright? Is there someone I can call to come over and be with you?" Julian asked. This was his first homicide; he wasn't sure exactly what to do with survivors.

"I am fine, I just need a moment," she muttered not picking her face up to look at anyone.

"Exactly what happened to her?" Mr. Osborne asked.

"We aren't sure at the moment. We have just started our investigation. This was found at the crime scene." Fiona took the ring out of her pocket once again and held it up for Mr. Osborne to look at. Tears started to well up in his eyes, this time he didn't even try to hide them. The realization that his daughter was dead was starting to sink in.

"That's my wife's ring. Felicity was infatuated with diamonds. She kept telling us they were a girl's best friend. She was having a sweetheart dance at her sorority last weekend and wanted to borrow it. She said it would bring her good luck. She was one of the girls nominated for Senior Sweetheart or something like that," her mother explained. "She was my little girl. We waited so long for her and now she's gone."

"I'm sorry ma'am, waited? What do you mean waited?" Julian asked, trying to be a part of this investigation now that he had gotten his foot out of his mouth and the embarrassment had subsided.

"We adopted her when she was ten years old. My husband and I do a lot of charity work. Twelve years ago, we were at an adoption agency fundraiser. These organizations have them every year to bring awareness to expectant mothers thinking about terminating their pregnancies and showing the benefits of placing their child up for adoption instead. While we were there, we saw this beautiful little girl, just adorable, sitting quietly playing with her dolls. I was instantly drawn to her. My husband and I have been very fortunate in the world of finance but even some things money can't buy. We tried for years but couldn't have a child of our own. This little girl was so sweet, I just knew we had to adopt her. We wanted to make her a part of our family. Since the day we brought her home she has been my life and the apple of her father's eye. There was nothing she asked for that Walter didn't provide." Mrs. Osborne explained noticing some of her balled up tissues were now in a pile on the floor.

"Do you know anything about her birth parents? Was Felicity taken from them because of abuse or neglect?" Julian asked making notes on his pad.

"Oh no, her biological parents were killed in a car accident when she was six. She had no other living relatives so she was put in a residential facility until she could be placed with an adoptive couple. How I wish we could have known sooner that she was there, we would have loved to adopt her right away but we never thought to ask. We inquired about a newborn but that wasn't in the cards for us. We love her detective, we raised her to be independent, respectful and hard working. She has a close circle of friends and was never in any kind of trouble. I just can't believe she is gone," Mr. Osborne said pouring himself another four fingers of scotch.

"We are going to need someone to make a positive ID of the body, but we can schedule that for tomorrow or the next day. Please call the station to make arrangements with the medical examiner when you are ready. It will take a few days before funeral arrangements can be made." Fiona left her business card on the liquor cart. "If you think of anything, anything at all please give me a call. Again, I am terribly sorry for your loss. My partner and I will see ourselves out." Fiona said walking toward the parlor's open doorway.

As they approached the car Fiona grabbed Julian by the arm. "Do you and I need to have a chat about being compassionate and respectful when it comes to making a death notification? You went after that poor man like he was a suspect without any proof that he was having a sexual relationship with the victim." Fiona reprimanded him like he was a child.

"No ma'am. I assure you it won't ever happen again. If it's any consolation, I felt like a complete ass." Julian said looking down at the ground embarrassed all over again.

"I know this is your first case but you need to stay calm, take your time, read each situation as it presents itself. You can't just assume and lead with accusations. Next time, follow my lead. I will make sure you have field time to brag to your friends about," Fiona said punching him in the arm. He winced but he hoped she didn't see him. He didn't want her to think he was a wimp.

"So, boss lady, what now?" Julian said still rubbing his arm. "Now, now we head over to the sorority and see who had a problem with our victim being sweetheart queen or whatever those sororities do," Fiona explained.

Seven

It had been a long day. The rain had started up again causing Fiona to get a chill deep in her bones. It wouldn't be long before her parka came out of the closet. She had given Julian the task of checking out the sorority their victim belonged to. No way she was going to be able to survive listening to preppy women in their twenties go on and on about life on sorority row. She just didn't have it in her today, plus Julian would be in his glories surrounded by all those women. He did look a lot like a lady's man. She was glad she was at least able to make the death notification. There have been cases when they haven't been able to make an I.D. for days. No parent, spouse or child should have to endure days of not knowing where their loved one is.

Fiona was on her way to visit her mother and couldn't help thinking about the Osbornes. That poor couple, longing all those years for a child of their own to stumble upon a little girl in desperate need of a home. Fiona wondered if Mr. or Mrs. Osborne ever thought about the idea of grandchildren. Don't all parents? Isn't that part of the plan? Your children have children and the love carries on?

Fiona suddenly felt a pang of disappointment. She would never give her mother a grandchild. It never really mattered to Fiona. She always believed she wasn't cut out for motherhood, but what if having a grandchild was something her mother longed for? Fiona knew it was still possible for her to have children, medically speaking, but in her mother's condition would she even be able to remember having a grandchild from one day to the next? This was another one of those times when she wished she had a sibling. Someone who could give her mother the one thing she may have always wanted.

In a lot of ways Fiona felt like a failure in her mother's eyes. It wasn't her fault that her mother got pregnant at such a young age, but she knew what her mother sacrificed to keep her daughter. She grew up watching her mother work endless odd jobs just to make sure Fiona had everything she ever wanted. The woman never tired. Her mother was working extremely hard to raise Fiona with the best of everything as if she were trying to make up for something. Right some wrong she had done in her past. Fiona often thought it was her, she was the wrong her mother had done. She was the sin of her mother. She never wanted to be a burden to her mother which is why she was having such a hard time dealing with the idea of her being in a home. Her mother was far too young to be trapped in a mind that doesn't remember some of the most important details of her life. Fiona wished things could be different. "I did what needed to be done to keep Mumma safe," she said out loud, willing the tears to stay tucked behind her eyes. She always got anxious and emotional when she went to visit. Her mother was her whole life. They weren't just mother and daughter. They were friends. There aren't many mothers and daughters who can say that.

The wind had picked up causing Fiona to use actual force to get the door open. A severe storm was still on the horizon. This weather brought her back to the night when she and Arthur were on the stake out. The night which changed how Fiona viewed life, being a detective, being a friend. A cold, windy, rainy night such as tonight. She hoped her mother was lucid when she arrived. She needed her. Her mom was her biggest supporter of her becoming a detective. She was there for her the night Arthur was shot and never left her side. She cried right along with Fiona curled up on the couch together as if Fiona were a little girl again, waking up from a bad dream.

"Hi Mumma! How are you?" she asked walking up to her mother gently kissing her cheek.

"Do I know you?" her mother asked looking so tiny in the jerry chair. Fiona scanned the room. Bed was made, no trash or dinner tray left on the table. Her mother's hair was combed nicely and she smelled of her favorite perfume. Fiona loved the smell of her mother's perfume. For what Fiona was paying for this place she was pleased to be getting her money's worth.

"It's me Mumma, Fiona. Do you remember me?" Fiona spoke loudly forgetting her mother wasn't deaf just senile.

"Oh Fiona, of course I remember you. You are my daughter. I would know that face anywhere. I just didn't recognize you with red hair. Did you have it done after school today?" her mother inquired beaming with pride that she remembered her daughter's name.

"No Mumma, I wasn't in school today. I am out of school. I am a detective now." Fiona explained. This was the normal routine whenever she visited her mother. Sometimes her mom would remember her but be confused as to what year it was, like today, or she would just stare off into space never knowing Fiona was even there.

"Well, you look awfully pretty today. Looks like you got your hair done. I see you got fresh flowers," Fiona mentioned walking over to the vase filled with purple and white flowers sitting on the windowsill. Fiona picked up the card and peeked inside. "Thinking of you today and always" the card read. There was no signature or name printed on the card.

"Any idea who sent these to you, Mumma?" Fiona asked knowing her mother may not even know the vase was here.

"Oh, the flowers? Those must be from Tim the gentleman in room 808. I think he has the hots for me," her mother replied winking at her daughter. If nothing else, Fiona was glad her mother still had her sense of humor, even if she didn't know she was making a joke, it still brought a smile to her mother's face.

Eight

The room smelled of the YMCA swimming pool with a mix of dirty sweat socks.

"Can't the department spring for a can of Febreze for this place? I have been to murder scenes that have smelled better," Detective Greyson yelled out loud, to no one in particular. He was a veteran detective and liked to play the man in charge around the office. Fiona wasn't in the mood to challenge his so-called authority and didn't feel like sparring with him this early in the morning, so she just walked past trying not to listen to his rant. She tapped her finger on her cell phone for the tenth time in almost the same number of minutes. Julian's text said he was five minutes away fifteen minutes ago. They were both being summoned to the M.E. office, but as usual Su Lee wasn't very forthcoming with info in her text. Fiona was about to leave for the morgue alone when Julian walked in holding a recycled paper tray with two coffees and a bag filled with what she hoped were donuts.

"You're late! Tell me there are donuts in that bag." Fiona said grabbing her coffee from the tray and flipping open the tiny plastic tab, blowing on the steam rising from the cup.

"Not only are they donuts, boss lady, but they are still warm. Hence why I am late, I waited for the next batch to be done so I could bring my leading lady fresh warm donuts," Julian explained raising his eyebrows up and down.

"Suck up" Fiona said rolling her eyes, walking towards the front door.

"What? Too much?" her partner shouted balancing the coffee and donuts while trying to keep up with her.

"You were late which makes us late, and I don't like to be late. We are needed at the morgue so move your ass!" Fiona said holding the door so he wouldn't trip.

"Thanks, how very nice of you to wait up for me." Julian said with a tone of annoyance in his voice.

"Don't kid yourself, I wasn't waiting for you I was waiting for the donuts," she said taking the bag from him and removing her hand from the door.

"Wow, someone took a bitchy pill this morning." Julian mumbled under his breath, yet thankful she didn't hear him. Clearly today was not the day to get on her bad side.

Even though the weather had cleared it was still chilly in Su Lee's office. Julian zippered his jacket a little higher. Su Lee looking annoyed said, "I can't do anything about the heat. If I put it up any higher the corpse will start to defrost and then you will complain about the smell."

What was with women today he thought to himself. Every woman he came in contact with this morning seemed to be pissed off about something. He put another mental check mark in the pro column as to why he thought it was a good idea to live alone, no one's moods to deal with.

"Can we just get to the reason you called us down here?" Fiona snapped. She too wasn't in favor of making small talk today. She didn't like the idea of a killer running around her city. She was starting to doubt if she had what it takes to be a detective. She knew she was being too hard on herself; she was a perfectionist and didn't like being forced to settle for anything less.

"The reason I asked you to come down here is because I have more information on your victim. Seeing as how you seem to have a short fuse I will get straight to the point. The finger isn't hers," Su Lee said matter of factly.

"Wait, what the hell are you talking about?" Fiona yelled at the medical examiner.

"My initial thought was the missing finger on the victim was the finger found in her mouth but after I performed some tests, I concluded that the finger found in the victim's throat was that of a man, approximately fifty-five to sixty years old. The finger was severed post mortem so whomever this finger belongs to is already dead." Su Lee explained.

"You have got to be kidding me?" Julian said outraged. "Is this a joke? Are you still pissed about me invading your space the other day?" Julian asked knowing how veteran employees of the force are always playing pranks on the rookies.

"I can assure you I wouldn't joke about a victim Julian. Having the lab put crazy glue in your Chapstick yes, we would all love a good laugh about that but never would I disrespect the dead by using them as a prank." Su Lee stated rather offended this insufferable idiot would think such a thing. "Where did you get this guy?" Su Lee asked Fiona, sounding sympathetic for her friend.

"Don't ask," Fiona said grabbing her coffee off the edge of the desk.

"I can't believe the finger doesn't belong to the victim. If it's not her finger, then what happened to the missing one from her hand?" Julian asked still wondering how bizarre this case was getting.

"Who knows, maybe some type of sea life ate it. At this point I wouldn't rule anything out. I need to head back to the station and start looking at old case files. Whoever this man was could have been murdered. We could very well have our killer sitting in a jail cell as we speak," Fiona explained her adrenaline pumping rapidly.

"What do you want me to do?" Julian asked not sure if he was about to get his head bit off again. His batting average with women today wasn't very high.

"Drop me at the station and then head over to the hospital. Find Nurse Crane, she owes me a favor, tell her we need to know of any males in that age range coming in through the E.R. with a missing finger, that may point us in the right direction." Fiona instructed her green partner. "I saw that smirk. Finger. Point in the right direction. You need to start taking this job seriously. Stop acting like you are still in junior high," Fiona sternly advised.

"Sorry, I didn't mean anything by it. I will get over to the hospital and meet you back at the station." Julian said. Walking to the car with his head down he wondered if he was ever going to get his foot out of his mouth.

The station was in full swing when Fiona pushed through the double doors. She raised her badge so the officer at the metal detector could see she was authorized personnel. She thought about how much the world had changed where even a police station isn't safe anymore. After the racial riots and 9/11 it was hard to find anywhere where you were truly safe. Even now, this small town had a killer on the loose.

"So, what you are saying is, a dead girl was found yesterday with a finger sewed into her mouth but the finger wasn't hers?" Detective Greyson asked leaning back in his office chair.

"Yes, that's what I said. Now we need to see if any murders took place within the last month or so where a male victim was missing a finger. A pinky finger to be exact." Fiona ordered. She was ranked under Greyson and shouldn't be demanding anything from him, but her gut told her she was on to something. Arthur always told her to follow her gut.

"I will run it through the database and see what I come up with. I should have results in about fifteen minutes. In the meantime, sweetheart, why don't you make me a cup of coffee?" Greyson responded with arrogance dripping off his voice.

Fiona rolled her eyes. She hated the way some of the other detectives treated her. She was a good cop. She took the same detective's exam they did and passed with flying colors. She deserved to be treated like an equal, but after her situation with Arthur some of the men in this department took issue with her being a female detective. There were plenty of men left in the world that still believed women were still the inferior sex. Deep down she couldn't blame them. At least three times a day she wondered if she were better off becoming a lawyer, at least she was pretty certain she wouldn't kill one of her clients.

After twenty minutes, Greyson walked over to her desk. "Nothing in the database but I went ahead and checked the log for ambulance runs. Seems rig number four responded to a call regarding a bar fight where one of the offenders was wielding a knife. Report shows one man was brought into the hospital with two missing fingers. It's the closest I got for you." Greyson dropped a copy of the report on her desk. "Oh, by the way, thanks for the coffee," he said walking back to his desk not bothering to turn around.

"I know, I know, I am on it. Your friend Crane is getting me the medical report. Guy's name was Winston Ferreira. He was in his late fifties. Didn't even make it out of the ambulance. He was a d.o.a. Seems he was involved in a bar room brawl and ended up with a broken beer bottle in his abdomen," Julian yelled into the phone.

There was a lot of commotion going on in the emergency room causing Fiona to have trouble hearing him with all the background noise. "Yeah thanks, I will see you when you get back here," Fiona yelled back, not sure if he even heard her.

Nine

"I can't understand who could have leaked the finger Captain. The only people who knew we were following up on the severed digit was Julian, Su Lee, and Greyson. Julian spoke to a nurse at the hospital but I am certain she wouldn't have talked to the press. I trust her enough to know that much," Fiona explained seeing the fury in Captain Braga's eyes.

The Captain didn't like his cases splattered across the front page of the local papers unless the words "in custody" were printed in bold letters.

"You need to stay on top of this Fiona. You wanted a case; I gave you one. Don't make me regret it." The captain knew he had hurt her which wasn't his intention. He didn't mean to. Luckily Fiona was wearing a thick skin. Something Arthur told her was a necessity if she wanted to become a good detective.

"There is always going to be someone who thinks they could have performed an investigation better, solved it sooner, or quicker. Don't let anything or anyone break your focus. When you work a case, it becomes your every breath. Nothing else will matter until the case is closed," Arthur used to advise her. He was always forthcoming with whatever wisdom he could impart to her. She missed him. He was as close to a father she was ever going to get and he was gone.

"I promise, there is no way this leak came from my people. All the officers know it's against the rules to talk about any investigation with civilians. I will have a word with them and remind each one there will be hell to pay if I find out someone is talking outside these walls," Fiona explained to her superior.

"I know last year was very difficult for you. If I didn't think you were capable of handling this case, I wouldn't have assigned it to you. Arthur always said you had something special, that you could crack even the hardest case if you just had a little more experience. He had the utmost confidence in you as I do. I know you are going to catch this son of a bitch," he explained to her. He wanted to see her make peace with what happened last year, but he could see she was still carrying it around with her and it made him uneasy.

"Julian, please tell me you didn't talk to anyone other than Nurse Crane when I sent you to the hospital today?" Fiona asked accusingly.

"No, I spoke only to her. She was rather crazed and I had to keep up with her as she was sprinting up and down the halls but I didn't speak to anyone else. There were people everywhere. A school bus filled with cheerleaders and the entire football team, overturned on the highway. Kids were crying, parents were freaking out. It takes a special type of person to work in the medical field, I know I couldn't do it," he explained to her.

She wanted to believe her partner but there was something about him. She couldn't quite figure it out but something about him seemed off. She didn't have time to stew on that, she had a killer to catch.

"OK, so what do we know?" Fiona asked. The more she went over the facts the more she hoped something would click in her head. Julian walked over to the white board that was now set up in a make shift conference area in one of the old interrogation rooms.

"The victim's name is Felicity Osborne, adopted by Linda and Walter Osborne at the age of ten years old. She was bounced from foster home to foster home until she got too old for any foster parents to take her in. Most want to take in an infant not a child. Spent six years in, well, basically an orphanage, until Linda Osborne met her twelve years ago and decided she wanted to adopt her.

She graduated the top of her class in high school. Missed out on being valedictorian by three points. Went on to the local University where she excelled in all her classes, maintained a three-point nine GPA, and was just crowned Sweetheart Queen at Delta Si. I talked to all of her sorority sisters and not one had a bad word to say about her.

She didn't have a steady boyfriend. She focused on her classes and other than her sorority sisters she didn't have any other friends. No one knows how or why she was at the beach. Everyone at the sorority house thought that she was in her room studying," Julian flipped his notepad to the next page and continued.

"Her body was found washed up on shore at roughly 4:15 a.m. yesterday morning. M.E. hasn't given a definite answer on time of death yet. Su Lee thinks her body was in the water for several days. Waiting on tests results to narrow down actual time of death. Based on the length of time she was in the water it's plausible she wasn't killed on the beach. Victim's mouth was sewn shut, but inside was a severed finger enclosed in an evidence bag. The severed finger had a dark blue thread tied around it. The finger was initially thought to be that of the victim but confirmed it is that of a male approximately fifty-five to sixty years of age. From the information I obtained from your source at the hospital, a male fitting that age bracket was brought into the E.R. nine days ago, pronounced dead on arrival. According to the chart, the right-hand ring finger and pinky finger were severed off with a broken beer bottle. Someone had to have had one hell of a grip on that broken piece of glass in order to cut two fingers clean off."

"The dead man's name was Walter Burbank, well known at the local watering hole. Twice divorced, no children, worked odd jobs on and off, but was more of a fan of the unemployment checks than working for a living. His body was taken from the morgue by Fitzgerald's funeral home. According to what I can get on line, there was no wake and no funeral, his body was cremated. I am waiting for a call back from the funeral home to set up a time to talk to the director. I am curious as to whether or not the funeral home was in possession of the body with his severed fingers or if the hospital "misplaced" them."

Julian took a breath. He had just recited everything he knew about the case. He was actually quite proud of himself. He was detailed and even threw in his theory about the funeral home at the end of his speech.

"The only thing we have to go on right now is the funeral home. Good work Julian," that was all Fiona offered. She was stumped. She needed something tangible to work with. There had to be something she was missing.

"Do we know anything about Walter Burbank, other than the fact that he was a steady customer at the bar?" Fiona questioned Julian, slowly sipping her coffee, which tasted like hot mud. She made a mental note to bring in a Keurig, the squad room coffee was eventually going to give her an ulcer.

"All we know is what I told you. His address is in the file. He lived alone but he did have two ex-wives. Possible he was behind in alimony payments and one of them figured she would rough him up in front of his drinking buddies?" Julian suggested knowing he was reaching for ideas.

"Only one way to find out, grab your coffee Julian we are going to the bar," Fiona said, grabbing her keys and making her way to the front door again.

"It's five o'clock somewhere." Julian said, shrugging his shoulders.

Ten

The bar was empty which wasn't unusual for this time of the day. Most lifers of the bar stool weren't awake before noon and today was no exception. The woman behind the bar looked as though she wore a shine on a bar stool or two back in her younger days. Her hair was almost completely white if you didn't take into account the yellow nicotine hue at the base of her hairline just above her forehead.

Fiona and Julian took a seat at the corner of the bar. The woman slid two flimsy cardboard coasters across the bar, one almost falling onto the floor if Julian didn't catch it in time. "Nice catch cutie, what can I get you?" she said. Fiona interrupted the bartender's flirtatious intro by sliding her badge onto the bar.

"We need to ask you some questions about an incident that happened out front a little over a week ago involving a man by the name of Walter Burbank. Does that name sound familiar to you?" Fiona whispered leaning into the middle of the bar propped up on her elbows. Not that it mattered, there wasn't anyone in the place to overhear them.

"Walter? Yeah, I knew him. He was a regular. Had been for years before he died. Poor Bastard." The bartender said wiping the counter with a dirty white towel. This place was a far cry from a respectable establishment.

"Why is he a poor bastard?" Julian asked, concerned where that white towel had been.

"Because of that woman, she was insane that night. She was screaming and yelling at him to admit who she was to him. She too was drunk as a fart but it wasn't the first time those two had a go around. And the name is Rita, sweetheart," the bartender replied to Julian as if she had a chance in hell of going home with him.

"So, this woman, was she a regular as well? Do you happen to know her name?" Julian asked, now it was his turn to lean into the bar. Fiona was fine with him taking the lead. If she needed to use her partners good looks to get info, she wasn't above it.

"She came in from time to time. She was always looking for Walter. She made a point to ask if he had been in whenever she first arrived. She sat right there where your buddy is sitting, Walter's seat was the next one over. See the plaque on the back of the chair? All the boys chipped in and dedicated that chair to him after he died. Figured it was better than sending flowers to one of his ex-wives," Rita explained tossing a bucket filled with ice into the small freezer underneath the bar.

"Were her and Walter dating? Could their argument have been about their relationship?" Julian inquired. This could be a simple lover's quarrel turned deadly, the real question, who is this woman?

"Dating, yeah, that couldn't be further from the case. She was far younger than him. I am not sure what their relationship was but I can assure you it wasn't romantic," Rita replied rolling her eyes. Julian sensed some jealousy at the idea of Walter and this mystery woman being connected romantically.

"You wouldn't happen to know her name or anything about her other than her fascination with Walter, would you?" Julian asked this time winking at her trying to coax out any information she may have thought to keep private.

"The only thing I know is Walter wasn't into her romantically. He made small talk with her but he wasn't into her like that. She looked to be in her thirties, drove an army green jeep with Alaska plates, and liked to toss back beers right along with the fellas. Never did come across a woman who could match the number of long necks the boys could put away but she did. Most women her size would be wasted long before she was," Rita said walking down the bar to wait on an actual customer.

"Alaska plates? Do people really bring their cars here from Alaska? If so, it would have to be on a boat. Shouldn't be hard to trace seeing as how there can't be that many army green Jeeps coming in from Alaska. Want me to check it out boss lady?" Julian asked but Fiona was lost in thought.

What was the connection between Walter Burbank and this mystery woman? What did she want him to acknowledge? Whatever it was made her upset, outraged to the point she used a broken beer bottle to teach him a lesson. "Yeah, check out the Jeep, I am going to pay a visit to the most recent former Mrs. Burbank. I'll catch up with you back at the precinct." Fiona replied driving off in the Crown Vic leaving Julian standing stranded on the sidewalk.

The doorbell rang again. Fiona could hear someone moving around inside. The house was located at the bottom of a dead-end street. A light mocha colored house with black trim and a black porch. The lawn was well cared for and the driveway had a new Lexus parked next to a Range Rover. Whatever happened to Walter didn't leave his latest ex-wife worrying where her alimony payments were. She clearly didn't need the money.

"Just a minute," a labored breathing voice, from inside the house said. Fiona sensed the woman on the other side of the door may be in distress. She unsnapped the lock on her gun holster, never knowing what could happen once the door was open. Arthur taught her to be ready for any situation. "Things can go from calm to hostile in the blink of an eye. You always need to be at the ready," he used to tell her whenever he sensed she was letting her guard down. If only she had taken his words seriously that night last year, she wouldn't be standing at the door by herself.

"Sorry about that, I was doing yoga and didn't want to give up with only four minutes left." The woman stood in the doorway with a towel wrapped around her neck and sweat stained yoga clothes. Fiona wasn't a fan of yoga but she knew it was the latest fad.

"Not a problem Mrs. Burbank, my name is Detective Mitchell. I need to talk to you about your ex-husband," she instructed showing her badge to the widow in the doorway.

"Please come in, call me Shelia Wilcox. I went back to my maiden name when I divorced that piece of shit. Rest in peace of course." Miss Wilcox clearly had no love lost for the dearly departed. "What can I do for you detective?" Shelia asked.

"First let me say that I am sorry for the loss of your ex-husband, piece of shit or not. The reason I am here is there seems to have been a woman who was friendly with Walter at the bar in town. Would you happen to know anything about that?" Fiona asked.

"This again, I told Walter every time he called to stay away from that whack job. She was just out for a quick payday," Sheila said with some force in her voice, getting aggravated with the conversation.

"What makes you think she was out for money. From what I have been told he wasn't a man of means." Fiona said respectfully.

"Oh, he was of means alright. When him and I married I was stupid enough not to insist on a pre-nup. He walked away with a rather large settlement from my father's business. Before we divorced Walter worked with my father buying several local convenience stores. He made millions. I never realized how lucrative convenience stores were. My father and Walter cleaned up. During our divorce he threatened to sue my father's company for his share. Walter was an employee, nowhere was it stated in his employment contract that he was a shareholder in any of the stores he helped obtain."

Shelia blew out a frustrated breath. Fiona knew there was more to the story so she just sat on the couch patiently waiting for Shelia's story to continue. "My father decided it was best to pay off my ass of a husband than deal with a legal battle. By this point it was well known that Walter had a drinking problem. My father made sure Walter signed paperwork agreeing to a monthly stipend instead of a one lump sum, that way Walter couldn't try to threaten me with another lawsuit when he drank away all his money. My father planned to retire shortly after we divorced and wanted to make sure I was protected from Walter. My family figured with his drinking habits he wouldn't be long for this world, but never did we think he would have been murdered over a woman like that." Shelia continued to explain her marriage to Walter.

"Miss Wilcox, where does this woman fit into all of this?" Fiona asked not wanting to push but needing to keep her focused on the reason for her visit.

"Oh yes, the woman. Late last year Walter left a voicemail on my phone. I hadn't heard from him in a couple years. Said something about a woman who claimed to be his daughter. Said she was chatting him up at the bar and one word led to another. He truly believed that he may have been her father. Too much scotch will do that to a person, I guess, but that was years before I got involved with him. Naturally I assumed she thought he was loaded. The divorce and his meaningless threats made the business section of the local paper back then. Women all over the world have nothing better to do than plan their next con. It wouldn't have been hard to link the Walter from the convenience store scandal, which is what the papers called it, to the Walter that was permanently fixed to that grungy bar stool."

Shelia finally answered the one question that had been nagging Fiona all day. It wasn't much to go on but at least she knew this murder could have in fact been a crime of passion.

"You wouldn't by any chance happen to know her name, would you?" Fiona asked delicately.

"I wish I did; I would love to meet her and shake her hand. She saved my family a bundle killing that worthless ex-husband of mine, not another check will be sent to that low life alcoholic," Shelia replied with excitement in her voice.

"I appreciate your time Miss Wilcox. If you think of anything else please don't hesitate to contact my office." Fiona instructed handing Shelia her business card.

"Julian, I think I may have something. I am going to swing by the morgue on my way back to the station." Fiona left a message on her partner's voicemail. She wasn't sure where he was but she wasn't about to be derailed. She needed to talk to Su Lee and see if there was anything that could be done about the pinky finger in the medical waste bag. If the bag was taken from the hospital or the funeral home there may still be a chance there was DNA from the killer still on it. She crossed her fingers hoping this could be the break she was waiting for. She looked down at her hand holding the steering wheel. She couldn't help but think about Walter Burbank all alone in the morgue missing two fingers. Fiona wondered what happened to Walter's ring finger. Why would someone only take one of the fingers?

Traffic was insane due to never ending construction on the highway. Fiona couldn't understand why D.O.T. wanted to shut down two lanes of the highway to repaint the double solid line when it could just as easily be done at night when there were far less cars on the road. She shook her head and put on her red flashing light. She wasn't responding to an emergency but at this point she needed to get to the morgue before Su Lee left for the day. She didn't want to waste any time on her theory. Not to mention the flashing red light was another perk of the job. Her gut told her she was on to something.

She heard Arthur's voice in her head. He sounded so close, like he was sitting right next to her in the passenger seat. "Always follow your gut."

Su Lee wasn't in her office when Fiona arrived at the morgue. "Damn it!" Fiona cursed out loud. An orderly was pushing a gurney, the body completely covered with a sheet.

"You looking for Su Lee?" he said slowing down.

"Yeah, any idea where I can find her?" Fiona asked leaning up against the wall, not wanting to get in the way of the person on its way to a steel refrigerated drawer.

"She flew out of here about thirty minutes ago, heard her say something about another body being found. I have no idea when she will be back but she asked me to keep an eye on things while she was gone. Not sure what she was expecting me to see, all these guys are dead. They won't be any trouble," the orderly snickered. Before the words were even passed his lips, he turned the corner with the gurney to push through the double doors and the corpse's hand slid out from under the sheet. Fiona jumped a mile. She was on edge. She urgently wanted to talk to Su Lee.

"If you hear from her, let her know I stopped by." Fiona said sliding her business card into the pocket of the orderly's scrub shirt.

"Sure thing. I will leave a note on her desk with your card just as soon as I get this here fella on ice," he said with a chuckle. Fiona was grateful Arthur wasn't with her. He had no patience for people who disrespected the dead.

Eleven

The room was dark, the small table lamp strained to illuminate the entire room. She could barely see straight across to the bathroom but it didn't matter. All she needed to see was right in front of her. The newspaper. The article about the body that washed up on shore. This was all coming together. Her master plan was starting to take shape. Excitement raced through her veins. She could feel her blood pulsating. She needed to stay calm. Her plan wouldn't work if she rushed it. There was an order to these things. Slow and steady wins the race.

She laid back on the twin mattress, no sheet underneath her body. The room was cold but she felt her body tingle with warmth. She thought back to how all of this started, how her life was before she knew the truth. Before she realized she was abandoned. Left to die alone. She had heard people say that a mother becomes a mother the moment she finds out she is pregnant. She knew her mother never felt that way, her mother was different. Her mother threw her away.

Zayna couldn't remember the details of her life before the age of five, and those are memories she wished she could forget, though she still silently prayed her mother would come back for her. Patty Montgomery had been her social worker for as long as she could remember. She was the closest thing to a mother Zayna had, and that wasn't necessarily a compliment. Patty had left the office to take a private phone call. Zayna assumed the phone call was her loving husband asking if he should start dinner, or her perfect son calling to tell her he hit a home run at his baseball game today. Just the idea of a loving family, a place to belong, made her clench her fists into a tight ball.

Zayna stared at the framed family photo her social worker had on her desk. Each one looked so happy, large smiles painted across their faces. "It's not fair, why does she get to have a family and I don't? What makes her better than me?" Zayna thought, her eyes boring a hole into the photograph. Being stressed, exhausted and overworked, as many social workers were, Patty hadn't taken the time to lock the drawer containing all her case files. Zayna, wanting desperately to know where she came from, helped herself to the secrets in the green metal filing cabinet. The feel of the cold steel on her fingers didn't faze

Zayna. Her fingertips flipped past file after file, none of them of any interest to her until she saw the one she was looking for. ZAYNA ONYX MORGAN.

The answers she longed for were right inside the brown folder now sitting on her lap. Her hands were shaking, her entire body went cold. She wasn't sure if she was ready for the truth but knew it was now or never; Patty could return from her phone call at any minute. Zayna opened the folder, running her fingers up and down the page. There it was in blue ink. "Mother terminated all rights to Baby B Mitchell." In her mind she read an entirely different sentence. "Mommy didn't love you, didn't want you." From that point forward at the young age of twelve years old, she convinced herself she was damaged goods. Never would she feel worthy enough for anyone or anything. Alone in a world full of people and all she longed for was a mother to love her, to hold her, and kiss her boo-boo's better. What she ended up with was far less a fantasy and more of a nightmare. She had been bounced from foster home to foster home from the moment she wasn't a patient at the Barton Hospital. Zayna promised herself, at that precise moment, sitting alone in her social worker's office, that she would make her birth mother pay for throwing her away.

Twelve

There was an eerie quiet surrounding the nursing home tonight. No one roaming the halls, no chatter among the residents, the only noise was coming from her mother's room. It sounded like she was having a panic attack. Fiona picked up the pace and sprinted to her mother's room, not wanting to cause a disturbance to the other patients sitting in their chairs watching the nightly news. She wanted to get to her mother's room and assess the situation. Bethany had never been a bother other than her first few nights, which was to be expected. Dementia patients don't handle change well. They respond better to their normal routine. A new room, new bed, plenty of new faces can cause someone like her mom to become combative. Within a week, Bethany had grown accustomed to her new surroundings and the new routine. She didn't cause trouble or misbehave in any way, which is why hearing her mother yell was concerning to Fiona.

"Mom? Mom? I am here, settle down, everything is fine. Would you mind letting me through?" Fiona was talking to her mother and the nurses all at once. She didn't like seeing her mother upset. It wasn't something she was used to. Bethany had always been a calm and patient woman. It took an awful lot to get her feathers ruffled but right now she was inconsolable.

"Oh Fiona, thank heavens you are here. They won't let me see her; they took her away. Why won't they let me see her? It's been so long since I was able to see her. I can't believe she came all this way." Bethany could barely catch her breath she was talking so fast, her eyes as wide as saucers.

"Mom, you need to calm down. Please just sit back and take slow deep breaths." Fiona slowly mimicked how she wanted her mother to breathe while taking a glance around the room. Nothing looked out of place. The bed sheets were askew across the bed which was unusual since it was barely seven o'clock. Was her mother looking for something or did she tear the sheets off the bed out of pure frustration?

Fiona's heart felt heavy. She wanted to protect her from the world but knew she was fighting a losing battle. Her mother wasn't going to get any better, each day bringing more fear into both of their worlds. She wasn't sure which was worse, loving someone who can't remember who you are or never knowing you ever loved that person? She was certain she wasn't the first to ask themselves such a question. Early onset Alzheimer's was on the rise in the U.S. No one could determine the cause but it was much more prevalent than it had ever been.

After the nurses were able to get her settled in her chair, all but one left the room. She stayed just in case Bethany had another episode. She stood at the far end of the room looking out the window, wanting to give Bethany and Fiona as much privacy as possible.

"Mom, do you know who I am?" Fiona asked.

"Yes, Fiona, you are my daughter. Always have been, always will be." Bethany replied looking like her daughter had asked her a stupid question.

"Did someone hurt you?" Fiona tried again. She had read somewhere that people take advantage of alzheimer's patients because no one would ever believe what they say.

"Fiona, you are a police woman, who in their right mind would ever think to hurt me, knowing what you do for a living," she responded. Fiona smiled inside. Her mom not only knew who she was but also knew her occupation, this was a good start.

"Did you hurt anyone, mom?"

Bethany just rolled her eyes at her daughter and made a swatting motion with her hand. Fiona just laughed. She knew her mom wouldn't hurt anyone.

"If no one hurt you then what has you so upset tonight?" Fiona took both of her hands into her own. She looked into her mother's eyes kneeling down in front of her. Instantly a look of panic washed over her mother's face.

"You didn't see her, did you?" Bethany asked her tone as serious as ever.

"You mean the nurses? They have all left except for Keisha, she is over by the window." Fiona explained.

"Not the nurses, the woman, she was here just a few minutes before you got here. I was so happy to see her. I wanted you to meet her, but the nurses came in and I think they scared her off," Bethany said, her voice trembling. Was it fear or sadness in her voice? Fiona couldn't tell.

"Mom, there was no one here but the nurses when I came into the room. Who is this woman you saw?" Fiona asked wondering who her mother could be referring to.

"I didn't just see her, I talked to her. She said she had been waiting a long time to meet me and was really nervous I would be upset she found me." Bethany explained, this time when she spoke, she was getting frustrated all over again.

"It's okay mom, maybe she will come back to visit you again," Fiona said wanting to play along with her mother's fantasy. She didn't want her mother getting worked up again.

Fiona had just started to comb her mother's hair when she heard her cell phone chime. She looked at her phone and saw two messages from Su Lee and one from Julian. She wondered how she hadn't heard them before, but realizing the commotion she walked into when she first got here it was no wonder she didn't hear it. The messages from Su Lee and Julian were similar. She was needed at another crime scene. She didn't want to leave her mother now that she was calm but she didn't have a choice.

"Bye Mom, I will be back in a day or two. Please know how much I love you," she said kissing her mom on the top of her head.

"See you later Alligator," was all her mother said as she walked out the door.

"Miss Mitchell! Miss Mitchell, can I speak with you for a moment?" the voice came from down the hall. Fiona quickly turned around; she didn't have time to waste but she didn't want to be rude to the nurse who was now fast approaching her.

"I am so sorry I am in a bit of a rush, is this something we can talk about later?" Fiona questioned the nurse looking at her watch. The texts came in over forty-five minutes ago. She knew another round of texts would be coming in any minute. She prayed that Julian would be able to handle things until she got there. In her mind she made a list of all the things she hoped Julian would take care of; securing the crime scene, talking to witnesses, keeping the press as far away as possible. Her nerves started to get the best of her.

"Of course, I just wanted to talk to you about your mother and the incident that happened this evening. Call me when you have time, I am here until midnight. The name's Marjorie," the nurse said catching her breath from speed walking across the entire unit just to catch up to Fiona.

"I will, sorry but I really have to go. Take care of my mother for me," she said as she pushed her way through the entrance door.

Thirteen

Julian saw Fiona approach the scene. She waved her badge in the face of some nameless officer in uniform, bending down to pass beneath the yellow crime scene tape. The weather was warmer today, unseasonably warm for this time of year. Thankfully it wasn't raining, Fiona needed a homicide where actual evidence could be collected.

"Oh, thank God you are here. I thought I was going to have to send out a search party for you. I can't handle this kind of stress. The press alone are vultures. I couldn't walk by without one of them shoving a microphone in my face. Don't worry boss lady, I didn't make a peep. Didn't even bother to say 'no comment'. Brace yourself, Su Lee is in a foul mood. Where the hell have you been anyway?" Julian snapped at her glancing down at his watch to check the time.

She knew he was stressed based on the beads of sweat gathering on his forehead, but he sounded as if he were about to come unglued. She couldn't blame him. His first few days in homicide and she leaves him to fend for himself.

"Sorry Julian, I had a situation with my mother. I couldn't get to my phone. I didn't mean to throw you to the wolves, and by that, I mean having to deal with Su Lee on your own. Been there, done that," she said jokingly trying to calm his stress level.

"Yeah well, you'll get my therapy bill." He quipped right back. They were starting to get into a flow on how to read each other which made working together in high stress situations a little more tolerable.

"So, what's happening here, I saw the flashing lights from a mile away, this one must be a massacre." Fiona mentioned while putting on her rubber gloves.

"According to the responding officer the body was found on the front lawn, just sprawled out for the neighbors as if she were a lawn jockey. Honestly it looks as though she was put out on display." Julian was flipping through his notebook.

"Before we get into this you may want to get a new notebook. Spiral notepads aren't a good choice. If this killer is caught, and I promise you we will catch them, they are going to have defense council. First thing they are going to try to get tossed out is your notebook. They will claim pages were torn out, evidence to establish their client's innocence was removed from the murder book. Flat edged memo books work the best. Just a little trick I learned on my first case." Fiona said thinking back to when she was as green as him.

Arthur taught her all the tricks of the trade. What she would give to have him here with her right now. She felt more confident when he was around. He was her safety net. Now, she was not only flying solo, she was responsible for Julian and he wasn't much help keeping her calm and focused.

Just as Julian had described, the body was laid out on the front lawn, with multiple stab wounds to her neck and torso. There were so many she couldn't count them all. She couldn't even keep track of the ones she had already counted. This poor woman was covered in slices, and blood. Fiona had never seen so much blood before. Some weren't deep which told Fiona this was done out of rage, maybe even passion. This murder was personal. A large gash was open on her belly. Whoever this woman was had put up a fight. Her hands were crossed in front of her face, left over right. Thin stab wounds were trailing down her arm to her elbow, some of the blood already starting to dry onto her skin. Her entire body was covered in blood. "Who could do such a thing?" Fiona asked.

"Oh, how nice of you to show up. Hope this didn't pull you away from anything important?" Su Lee said in a sarcastic tone. Julian had warned her about Su Lee's attitude tonight but didn't think it would be aimed directly at her.

"Sorry, had an issue with mom." Fiona replied thinking it best to keep her excuse short and sweet. Su Lee gave her a sympathetic glance. She didn't know the details of her mother's current condition but she had heard through the office grape vine Fiona was struggling with her mother's illness.

"Anything of interest?" Fiona asked squatting down next to the body wanting Su Lee to change the look on her face. Fiona wasn't one for pity. "I see someone carved her up real nice. Anything you can tell me yet?" Fiona asked preparing herself for another sarcastic comment.

"Female, approximately thirty years of age, cause of death, stab wounds, obviously. Won't know which stab wound was the fatal cut until I get her to the morgue but my money is on the belly gash. Has to be about four or five inches deep. She certainly could have bled out from that one alone. I have no idea why the killer went to the trouble to slice her up but that's more your job than mine detective." Su Lee replied with the same tone as before.

"Do you have a time of death?" Fiona asked with a raised eyebrow.

Su Lee was upset about something. She never took these cases personal but her tone was a clear indication she was struggling to keep her emotions from rising to the surface.

"Best guess right now, I'd have to say between three and six p.m. this evening. But you haven't seen the worst of it. Come over here." Su Lee said standing to stretch her legs. Fiona followed her to the back of the medical examiner's van. It always amazed her how Su Lee could drive one of these vehicles. They weren't huge but she was so short barely touching the line of five foot it was a wonder how she reached the pedals.

"Brace yourself." Su Lee grabbed hold of an evidence bag, this time instead of a finger there looked to be a stuffed animal inside. The interior of the bag was so smeared with blood it was hard to make out what the exact animal was inside.

"Tell me there wasn't a child involved in this murder." Fiona asked, her voice tense. There is nothing worse than a cop being called to a scene when there is a child involved. Those cases had lasting power. Even if the killer were caught you can never get over the violent death of a child.

"I don't think so. Your insufferable prick of a partner spoke with the responding officer and there is only one body. Officers searched the entire area, according to him," Su Lee replied. This time she had a thickness to her voice as if she were fighting back tears.

"So, what's with the stuffed animal?" Fiona asked herself out loud.

"There are actually two, identical crocodiles. When the body was discovered these stuffed animals were laying on top of the victim's stomach," Su Lee said this time a single tear escaping from her eye. "Before you ask, the victim wasn't pregnant. From what I can tell she never had been. I will know more after I get a good look at her." Su Lee said wiping the tear off her face hoping Fiona didn't notice.

Su Lee was as tough as they come. In her line of work, she had to be. She saw more than any detective, spent more time with victims than anyone else, even if they were no longer alive.

"Keep me posted," was all Fiona said as she patted her friend on the shoulder and turned to find her partner. Fiona pretended not to notice Su Lee's tear, no need to embarrass her.

"It was awful, Fiona. I never saw anything like this. I may not be cut out for homicide. I may want to look into getting a job with Internal Affairs," he said sounding like he too was going to breakdown any minute.

"This is right where you need to be. Trust me, when we find the son of a bitch that did this, and I promise you we will, you won't feel the way you do right now. Justice will be served and you will know what it feels like to bring closure to whomever her loved ones are."

Julian didn't want to cry in front of Fiona so he flipped open his notebook and started rattling off what he already knew. "Victim is Amelia Leach, early thirties, single. Neighbor, Geoffrey Souza, found her when he pulled into the driveway from work this evening around six thirty. Naturally he is upset that this happened on his front lawn, but he is blaming himself. He thinks if he didn't stop to pick up dinner, he would have been home at his normal five o'clock and may have been able to save her. He said she lived three houses down. Nice woman, quiet, mostly kept to herself." "Mr. Souza said that she lived alone to the best of his knowledge. He said his wife may know more details but she is away on business, due to arrive home tomorrow afternoon."

"I told him that we would come back to speak with her. He was apprehensive about us talking to his wife. She had a miscarriage a few months ago and isn't handling it well. He asked that we don't mention anything about the crocodiles. Who would do this to another human being Fiona?" Julian said shaking his head, his lip quivering slightly.

The scene seemed quieter than normal. Usually there were officers everywhere asking questions, yelling out demands. Tonight, there was a hush on the street. Even the press was behaving. The situation had to be heinous to cause the press to keep quiet. This took everyone by surprise. The neighborhood was small, quiet, and family friendly. It had an old world feel to it. Fiona looked around, most houses had a basketball hoop in the driveway, bikes left lying on the lawn and swing sets in all the back yards. One even had a dog house that looked exactly like a smaller version of the larger house. This wasn't the type of neighborhood you would expect to find a dead woman laying naked a few houses from where she lived.

"What are you thinking boss lady?" Julian asked, fire in his eyes where there was nothing but somberness a moment ago.

"Have you blocked off the entire street?" she asked her partner, silently praying he did.

"Yeah, I sealed the entire street and put an officer at each corner to re-direct traffic. Why? I know there is something rolling around in that head of yours."

"We need flashlights and a couple officers. We need to walk along the street on both sides, and the lawn. She could have been attacked at home and ran, trying to get help. The killer may have caught up with her at the Souza's, or she could have just collapsed there. From what I saw, I don't' think she was running with those stab wounds but if so, there should be a trail of blood somewhere on this street or grass." Fiona explained feeling her own blood start to rush in her veins. Her gut was trying to tell her something.

"I had the boys take a look around while I was handling this on my own, waiting for you. They all seemed to be standing around until someone gave them instructions. C.S.U. has been working their way up the street for over an hour," Julian explained.

Fiona looked at her watch. "It's nine fifteen, according to Su Lee, the victim has been dead between three and six hours which is more than enough time for the killer to have gotten miles from here." Fiona looked frustrated.

"This doesn't look like a random killing. There has to be a connection between the victim and her killer. She was naked, stabbed so many times she looks like she went through a meat grinder. Sorry, that was in bad taste." Julian said, trying to not disrespect the dead. "Someone wanted her dead, and the victim knew it. She has defensive wounds up and down her arms. She could have been caught off guard. Maybe she came home from work and decided to take a hot bath and was surprised to find someone was in the house with her. She could have been sexually assaulted. The medical Examiner should be able to tell us that soon enough. Assuming she was able to overpower her assailant, she ran from the house, down the street to the Souza's. She may have known someone would have been home since it was nearly the end of the work day."

Fiona picked up where Julian left off, bouncing theories off her partner. This is how all investigations start, partners throwing out one hypothesis after another and seeing which one sticks. It's not as easy as that but you have to start somewhere. Fiona began walking slowly up the street to where the victim lived. If there was a struggle it had to have started there.

Fourteen

The uniformed officers were standing side by side trying to keep the press from trespassing onto the crime scene. The reporters at this end of of the street were much more aggressive than the mob located where the body was found. "Tony is lead for C.S.U. tonight," Julian said wanting to break the silent tension that was radiating between them.

"Got it, make sure you glove up and put on the booties, we don't want to contaminate the scene." Fiona instructed passing him a pair of rubber gloves.

"Wouldn't dream of it." He said, bending down to put on his booties. He wasn't being condescending. He couldn't have been more serious. This case was going to bother him for months to come. He couldn't get the image of the victim out of his head. He was one of the first on scene, even before the paramedics and fire department, he felt like he was the one to find her. Mr. Souza was standing in the driveway with his head in his hands. When Julian first approached the house, he could only see the body. It was as if nothing else existed, no grass, no mailbox or the lamp at the bottom of the driveway. Julian was just as stunned as Mr. Souza. He tried to clear his head but the image kept popping in like a scene from a horror movie.

"The house has been cleared. No sign of forced entry. Either the assailant came in through an open window or the victim knew who they were and let them in. A lover perhaps? We are taking the bed sheets to test for DNA and fluids. Whatever happened here it ended in a struggle. There is broken glass all over the bathroom floor. The wall length mirror was shattered. The victim put up one hell of a struggle," Tony explained but Fiona already knew everything Tony was reporting. She knew the moment she walked into the living room and saw the furniture over turned.

"Could it have been a robbery gone bad? Perhaps whoever broke in to steal didn't anticipate the owner coming home so quickly," Julian questioned. He was certain of only one thing at this point, anything was possible.

"Could be but again, no sign of forced entry. There are two points of entry and neither looked to have been tampered with." Tony said pointing to both the front and back door. The house was smaller in size than the rest of the houses on the block. Most of the houses look to have started off small but additions and remodeling were added later. This house however didn't look to have any major construction done to it.

Fiona made her way into the bathroom and the sight made her gasp. There was blood everywhere. It was splattered across one side of the wall; she could see the way it dripped down onto the floor and left a small sticky puddle. The mirror had been shattered just like the C.S.U. tech had mentioned.

"Julian!" she yelled into the other room. "Make sure every piece of glass is picked up and bagged as evidence," she continued to yell over her shoulder.

The bathroom wasn't very big, barely large enough to fit a tub, toilet and sink. Fiona looked inside the tub; it had a shine to it. She ran her gloved finger across the inner wall, noticing how slippery it was. It hadn't been that long since water was filled in the bathtub. More than likely some type of bath oil or bubbles were added to the water causing the shine.

"Tony, did you swab the tub? Seems to me there was water in it not long ago." Fiona continued to yell over her shoulder.

"Yes ma'am, we swabbed the tub and took some hair out of the drain. Doubt it will be anything but the victims but you never know." Tony yelled from the far side of the bedroom adjacent to the bathroom. Tension was high, you could feel it throughout the entire house.

"Fiona! I got something! Get in here!" It was now Julian's turn to yell. Fiona rushed into the bedroom and found Julian holding the victim's cell phone.

"It's locked but I think we can get the Technical Assistant Response Unit to unlock it for us. What are the chances she took a pic of her attacker?" Julian said with a slimmer of hope in his eyes.

"If only real live cases played out like they did in the movies Julian, we wouldn't need as many detectives on the force as we do." Fiona said rolling her eyes. She held the phone lightly by the sides not wanting to disturb any prints that may have been left on the phone.

"If she knew who her attacker was, there is a chance they could be in her phone. A picture, a message. We need to get this unlocked. Tony!" she was yelling across the house again.

"Yeah, I am right here." He stated from two feet behind her.

"Sorry, I didn't see you there. I need this bagged and sent directly to T.A.R.U. Tell the officer to go straight there and stand over Melissa until she gets this unlocked." Fiona instructed with a stern expression on her face. She was starting to get pissed off. She now had two bodies and no idea where to begin looking for the killer. This phone may be the only thing that can aid in her investigation. Fiona heard her cell phone vibrate in her pocket. There was a missed call from the nursing home. She stepped outside to listen to the voicemail. She wanted to make sure her mom wasn't having another episode.

"Hi Fiona, this is Marjorie, your mother is fine so please don't panic. She is actually sound asleep. Soon after you left, she went to bed, said she was exhausted which is normal after an upset like she had. I just wanted to touch base with you about the woman your mother said she saw. I saw her too. I know she was lucid when she told you about her. Call me when you have a chance. Have a good night."

Fiona exhaled, releasing the deep breath she was holding in. She was glad her mom was doing better. If she wasn't, she would have felt even worse having to leave her. She felt she never had a lot of time to spend with her. Time was the one thing her mother didn't have enough of.

At this hour of the night the press had gone home, they had gotten all they could for now but they will be in full force tomorrow, calling the station and standing out front waiting for someone to give them a statement. She looked out into the dark night, other than the house filled with police, the neighborhood was back to its normal quiet.

The sound of a twig snapping drew her attention to the side of the bushes over the fence in the adjacent yard. As Fiona approached, she saw a slender figure running down the street. The figure was dressed in what looked to be running gear. Too slim to be a man, the figure had on a knitted headband and the running sneakers had orange reflecting Nike swoosh marks on the side.

Fiona recognized the headband immediately. Her mother used to hand knit her one every year for Christmas. It was tradition for one to be sticking out of her stocking every Christmas morning. Unfortunately, her mother had forgotten how to knit and the head bands stopped appearing in her stocking. Fiona ran to the middle of the street hoping to get a better look but the figure was gone. Vanished as quickly as it had appeared.

Fifteen

The station looked different. Something was off. Where was everyone? The chairs in various cubicles still had sport jackets draped across the back. Detectives were still in the building, but where? She made her way past the empty desks to her own.

" What a mess," she thought to herself, unzipping her jacket to toss onto the back of her chair. Julian's desk was immaculate. Neatly stacked piles of manila folders were sitting on the edge of the desk, waiting for her signature she assumed. His pens were laying, by size, in an orderly fashion next to his computer's keyboard. He had tiny mesh bins lined up in front of the computer, each one containing a different sized binder clip. "Man, he has issues," she said to herself. Just as she was about to sit down she heard the Captain yell, "Mitchell! In my office, NOW." Whatever she was walking into wasn't an accolade for a job well done on the last night's crime scene.

"You rang Captain?" Fiona joked as she shut the door to his office. She was hoping to keep the mood light. She could tell by his tense stature that he wasn't sharing the same light hearted mind set.

"Have a seat Mitchell." He said in his formal Captain voice. When he spoke with such authority Fiona knew he was all business and the joking wasn't going to ease the tension in the office. Fiona sat up straight in the chair bracing herself for whatever was coming at her next. Instantly she thought of Arthur, he trained her never to relax when working a case. "When you relax, you get comfortable. Comfort equals mistakes. Mistakes are for the perpetrators. When Detectives make mistakes there could be someone's life on the line." He used to tell her all time.

Little did she realize it then but she learned her lesson the hard way. The last time she relaxed on a case she lost her mentor, the only person who treated her like a father should treat a daughter.

Half listening to what the Captain was saying, half in her own thoughts she jolted her full attention back to what she had just heard.

"Wait, you are taking me off the case? Captain with all due respect, I have been working this case since the body was found washed ashore a couple of days ago. You can't take me off this case. I have two victims, evidence I am waiting on from the lab. Please Sir, don't do this." Fiona pleaded fighting back tears. This was her one chance to have the colleagues in her department change their opinion of her and the Captain was taking it away. Pulling it right out from under her before she even had a chance to solve any one of the murders piling up.

"I am not taking you off the case. I am giving you a task force to help aid in your investigation. When this case involved the one body washed ashore, I had no doubt that you could handle it, but let's face it, this case has multiple victims and you can't work them all at once. I know you and your partner have been working night and day with no sleep. It's not healthy. Don't look at this as a sign of weakness or that I don't believe you to be an asset to the force, but you aren't wonder woman. There is no shame in having people to help you," the captain explained.

"I understand Sir." Even though she didn't. She didn't want help. This was her case and who the hell was he to take it away from her? She barely had a moment to catch her breath let alone catch what could possibly be a serial killer.

"I know you feel the need to prove something to the boys out there and to Arthur. You don't owe anyone, other than the families of the bodies in the morgue an apprehended killer. Stop being so hard on yourself. You are doing a great job. I have appointed you lead of the task force." The captain continued to explain stroking her ego just a bit to give her the confidence she lacked.

"There will be several familiar faces out there and a couple new ones."

"I understand Captain. I will play nice with the fellas as long as they are aware of who is in charge. This is my case and they need to follow my lead." Fiona stated as she walked out of the office closing the door with a little more force than was necessary. She was pissed and this 'task force' was going to learn quickly that she wasn't someone to push around.

Sixteen

She was sweating. The stains under her arms were proof this evening was a little too close for comfort. She knew she should have stayed away. She was sloppy tonight. It was obvious the detective would have come outside at some point. She wasn't going to stay in the dead woman's house forever. She should have known better. She should have been further away. It was her own salacious need to see them all scramble, trying to figure out who or what stabbed that poor woman. She believed in her heart that woman got what she deserved. She and the other one, the other blond. Anyone that got in her way was erasable. There was nothing she could do now but take a hot shower, hopefully calm her nerves and plan her next move. She didn't anticipate Julian being a part of the plan but he too was disposable. She was going to try to avoid hurting him at all costs, but if need be, she would be able to do it. She would be able to destroy the one man who has helped her since she came to town. Granted, he wasn't willing to help her at first, but everyone has their price. All in good time. Her plan was working. Fiona was starting to fall apart. These women were only the beginning. She had far more in store for Detective Fiona Mitchell.

Zayna learned about Fiona long ago. She had read the file over and over again. Anytime her social worker left the office she took a peek at the file inside the metal filing cabinet. Each and every time she learned more of her family heritage. Her mother was young, attractive and smart. Her boyfriend split when he found out he was going to be a father. Another one that abandoned her. At least he abandoned all of them and not just her.

Her mother was the one to single her out. How hard was it for her to choose one baby over the other? The space for 'father's name' on her birth certificate was left blank. Zayna was surprised her mother had the audacity to sign her birth certificate. Why put your name on something you have decided to throw away like an empty coffee cup on the side of the road?" Zayna thought to herself as she stripped off her running clothes and stepped into the steaming hot shower.

The more she thought about how awful her life was in comparison to her perfect sister made her scrub harder, so hard her skin started to sting with blotches of red appearing across her body.

Zayna had always felt dirty. She couldn't remember a time when she felt clean. Her foster homes weren't in the same neighborhood as Mr. Rogers. The majority of them were abusive, some sexual, some emotional. Whenever Zayna complained to her social worker she moved her in with a different family. The last name was the only difference from one home to the next. A pretty little girl was either beaten for being just that, or some male in the house used her for their own selfish needs. Either way, each house was the same.

Fiona was loved, Zayna was tormented. Life wasn't fair but she planned to even the score.

Seventeen

Fiona took a deep breath with her hand on the doorknob. Be assertive, forceful and above all be professional, she told herself as she turned the door handle. This was the moment she had been dreading. On the other side of this door were fellow officers, comrades, some she even considered friends but after last year she couldn't help but feel she was constantly being watched, judged, always under a microscope. In her mind, she pictured them all staring at her with raised eyebrows just waiting for her to screw up. She was certain no one would want to team up with her, which may explain how she got stuck with Julian. There were times when she considered herself damaged goods but the idea of everyone else thinking so was hard to bear.

She was looking for a reason to ditch Julian. In the beginning, when this was a simple one victim homicide, she could handle teaming up with a rookie detective, but things were different now. In the blink of an eye, she went from one body to two and she had a feeling whomever was responsible for these killings wasn't done yet. She needed a partner who didn't require constant supervision and hand holding.

In addition, there was still something about Julian that left a sour taste in her mouth. She knew he came from a political family, which was most likely how he got his shield, but it was much more than that. There was a secretive side to him, she could see it in his eyes. There were moments when she would look at him and feel as if he wanted to say something to her but wouldn't let the words come out of his mouth.

Before she had met Julian, she had prepared herself for a partner with an enormous amount of arrogance, instead she got a self-loathing meek man who seemed to constantly be looking over his shoulder. His paranoia was different from hers. Fiona's was based on being accepted by her peers, while Julian's paranoia seemed to stem from guilt.

"Good Afternoon All, if I could have your attention, we have a lot to cover. As you may know, my name is Detective Mitchell and I have been assigned lead detective on the case the media has now dubbed 'The Forget Me Not Killer'. There are several of you I know and some I haven't had the pleasure of meeting. I want to go around the room and have everyone introduce themselves. There is plenty of work to be done and now may be the only time we get to learn one another's name." Fiona took a deep breath hoping no one could hear the nervousness in her voice.

"I will go first. As I said, I am Detective Mitchell. I have been in homicide for almost five years. As some of you may know, I lost my partner last year. There have been speculations regarding my involvement or lack thereof surrounding the incident. If anyone has any questions or wants to confirm what has been floating around the rumor mill, now is the time to ask. We have a multiple murder investigation to solve with a possible serial killer on the loose but if you would prefer to waste my time with questions that won't bring my partner back let's handle it now. I will make sure to let the families of the victims know we will search for the killer when the gossip has ended."

Fiona liked this assertive side of her. She knew she would be up against a lot of stares, comments and snickering with this new task force but she was determined to let her fellow detectives know she wasn't going to be one to mess with.

The room was eerily quiet. No one spoke a word, until the only other female officer in the room raised her hand. "Yes, you there," Fiona said motioning for the woman to ask whatever question was on her mind.

"I am Detective Audrey Tavares. I have been on the force for over six years. Let me start by saying I am sorry to have heard about Arthur. He was loved around here by everyone. No one in this room is going to ask you any questions. We all know how easily we could all be put in a tough situation. We are here for one reason and one reason only, to catch a killer." Detective Tavares finished speaking and looked to Julian to be the next in line for introductions and glared at each person in the room making it known gossip wasn't going to sit well with her either. Fiona instantly knew she wanted to know more about Audrey. She got the feeling this woman was a no nonsense get it done type of detective.

"Hey guys, I am Julian. I just started in the Homicide Unit. This is my first case. I am learning as I go and honestly, I think it is all fascinating."

Fiona couldn't believe that was all he had to say. "What an idiot," she thought to herself. She needed to find someone she could pair him up with. She couldn't deal with this over grown teenager for much longer.

"I guess I am next. My name is Officer Daniels. I know almost all of you. Due to an injury I sustained a few years back, I am no longer useful in the field but I am your go to guy when it comes to anything technical. There were no spots open in T.A.R.U. so I stayed on as a Detective, mainly not to lose my pension. I am here for whatever you need Detective Mitchell." He finished speaking and looked over to the only person left in the room.

"I am Detective Dubois. I have been a Detective for over twenty years. I too had a similar situation as you did last year Mitchell so I know what you are going through."

Fiona took a deep breath; this may not turn out to be as bad as she thought.

Eighteen

Fiona held her head in her hands at her desk. She had been at the station for hours. The sun was starting to rise. She needed sleep. Her body was starting to ache, her eyes starting to blur with every blink. Coffee wasn't helping at this point. It was only making her jittery. She needed to start somewhere. She opened her desk drawer and heard the squeak of the metal sticking to the sides. The noise was worse than nails going down a chalkboard. She knew she needed to talk to Amelia Leach's former employer. Why would someone want to kill an attorney? Did she wrong a client? How were Amelia and Felicity connected? Did they both know the killer? Could Amelia have represented a man Felicity dated? She wrote that on her list but also made a note of the slim figure she saw running down the street with a large question mark. She was stuck on this. It seemed odd to her that someone would be out, in full track gear, running down the same street a murder had just occurred. Nosey neighbor or not, that took balls.

Fiona's' phone rang. The ringtone pulled her out of her thoughts. The caller ID showed the nursing home's number. She picked up the phone on the third ring, welcoming the distraction.

"This is Mitchell," she stated stifling a yawn.

"Fiona?" the woman on the other line asked. "Yes, is my mother alright?" Fiona answered holding her breath.

"Oh, my yes, she is fine, sleeping in fact. My name is Marjorie. I left you a message last night and hadn't heard back from you. Am I calling too early?" the woman asked speaking softly.

"No, I haven't been to bed yet. It's barely five a.m. You are up early for someone who worked until midnight," Fiona explained.

"I agreed to work a double shift so they gave me an extra hour break in order to get some rest. I was sitting in the break room and couldn't help thinking about your mother which prompted me to call you again." Marjorie sounded just as tired as Fiona.

"Yes, you mentioned something about my mother's episode last night." Fiona replied rubbing her eyes, it seemed much longer than just a few hours ago she was at the home with her mother.

"I know there are times when your mother isn't herself. We see it all the time here, but I assure you she was completely lucid last night. I saw the same woman your mother was talking about. Saw her with my own two eyes. Four if you count my contacts." She explained making a joke, clearly overtired.

"Who was this woman?" Fiona asked. She couldn't think of anyone that would visit her mother, other than herself and Mrs. Appleton.

"The woman had been in once before. She didn't see your mother the first time she was here. She only stopped at the nurse's station and inquired about your mother's health. She had quite a few questions about the care she was receiving, her eating habits and that sort. I wasn't the nurse assigned to your mother's room that day but I was at the station when she walked in. She reminded me a lot of you now that I think of it. She had hair just like you do. Anyway, the nurse on duty didn't give out much information. All she told her was your mother was in very good health other than the dementia," Marjorie explained.

"I have no idea who this woman is. Did she leave a name or number?" Fiona inquired sounding less like a detective and more a concerned daughter.

"No, not that I know of. She did ask if it were possible for your mother to leave the nursing home for a few hours. The nurse told her some of the patients leave for several hours during the holiday season but most of the time, families mainly utilize the gardens for afternoon visits when the weather is nice," Marjorie replied.

"I don't understand why this woman is so interested in my mother. She doesn't have any family to speak of. She was an only child just like me and I have never met either of my grandparents or my father." Fiona knew she was divulging too much info but she was exhausted and just started rambling.

"Last night when she came in your mother didn't recognize her at first, at least I didn't think so. The woman started talking to her and once she realized who she was, your mom went wild. She started to cry and was so happy to see her she started yelling like it was midnight on New Year's Eve. As you know your mother is a very quiet woman. A reserved woman who out of the blue starts to yell regardless of the reason causes concern for the staff. I was one of the last to arrive to her room. The woman was walking down to the end of hall waiting for the elevator to open. At that point, I didn't know what was happening or I would have stopped the woman." Marjorie said apologetically.

"Marjorie, please don't think I am blaming you or anyone for what happened. Mom was hysterical when I got there last night. She was upset that I didn't get to meet whomever had come to visit her. I was actually pleased to see her thrilled about something. I knew she was lucid. She knew who I was and what I do for a living. It assured me she was in her right mind. I will try to get by there today and see how she is. I hate to cut you short but I need to get back to work. Things are hectic around here." Fiona explained feeling bad that she couldn't continue her conversation with Marjorie who sounded like a really sweet woman who cared about her mother.

"Oh, honey you go take care of whatever you are doing. I heard about that poor woman found on the front lawn. It was just horrible what I heard on the news. I will call again if that woman comes back. Take care now." Marjorie said before hanging up the phone.

The television news stations had run the story, that didn't take long she thought to herself. She knew the Captain was going to want an update as soon as he got in. She just hoped she would have something to tell him. Before she put her phone down, she sent a text to Julian. He was checking in with T.A.R.U. before coming in this morning. "Any update? Bring coffee," she typed and hit send. "And DANISH," she added and hit send again. If he was going to be late, he should at least bring her breakfast.

Fiona walked out of the bathroom wiping her face with a stiff paper towel. The cold water woke her up more than she thought it would. As she turned the corner, bumping into Tony from C.S.U. Fiona was glad she wasn't the only one who looked like they hadn't slept in days. His clothes were wrinkled and his hair was disheveled.

"Wow, glad to see I am not the only one who looks like shit run over twice," he said.

"Always a pleasure to see you too Tony," she replied stepping aside to walk past him.

"I was actually on my way to see you. I have the initial reports from last night's homicide." He said, fanning his face with the manila fold. Fiona stopped midstep and reached for the folder, snatching it from Tony mid fan.

"Anything I should know?" Fiona asked opening the folder while walking back to her desk.

"There is something in there I think you will find rather interesting. The hairs we took from the bath tub drain didn't belong to just the victim." Tony said with a gleam in his eye.

"Really?" Fiona said flipping the pages in the file. "Thank you for putting a rush on these, I know you must have been up all night. I owe you one," she said sitting at her desk looking like she was about to start reading the next great American novel.

"Well, now that you mention it," Tony started to say but was interrupted.

"I am still not going out with you." Fiona said putting her hand up without even looking away from the file. Tony grabbed hold of his chest mimicking taking a bullet straight to the heart.

"We'll see about that," he said jokingly. "Call if you have questions. I am heading home for a shower and a nap. I will be back in a couple hours if anyone is looking for me." He turned to leave but Fiona didn't notice because she was nose deep in the file he gave her.

Nineteen

"I am on my way there now, make sure you get there as soon as you can. Call Melissa and tell her you need that phone unlocked. She is to work on nothing else until that is done. I will see you soon." Fiona yelled into the phone, weaving in and out of lanes of traffic at a faster pace than she was comfortable with. How can there be yet another victim? Whoever was responsible for the attacks on these women worked fast. She hadn't even talked to Su Lee about Amelia Leach yet. Fiona thought about how tired she was and then pictured Su Lee and the bodies that were stacking up in the morgue. She could outsource some of the autopsies but Fiona knew better than to suggest such a thing. The tiny medical examiner was almost as stubborn as Fiona was. Maybe she could have Julian mention it to her. He could get his head bitten off. It would at least give Su Lee a good laugh if nothing else.

Fiona could barely get her car parked before the press started hounding her.

"Detective, is this the work of a serial killer?" one asked. "How are women in this town supposed to feel safe with a killer on the loose?" another one said with a tape recorder shoved in her face.

"No comment," Fiona replied trying to push her way through the crowd. This must be how celebrities felt whenever they tried to go somewhere in public, she thought to herself. She was starting to get cranky and her fuse was getting shorter with every microphone aimed at her head.

"Is your partner's theory correct, are these the acts of a vigilante?" One reporter said causing Fiona to turn and stare at the woman holding the microphone inches from her face.

"What? No, well, we don't know anything definite as of yet. Please do not cause mass hysteria with assumed theories. The Captain will be holding a press conference later today to address the people of this town. Please let me through," she demanded. Fiona looked at the woman and noticed long red hair draped in front of her shoulders, her perfect make-up and wool coat. Reporters were always dressed classy in case they ended up going live in front of the cameras.

Fiona finally walked onto the scene and was taken aback by what was directly in front of her. A woman, roughly the same age as the previous two victims in the front seat of a blue Volvo with a screwdriver lodged in her neck. The paramedics were entering through the trunk trying to secure a way to transport the patient without further injury. "She is still alive?" Fiona asked one of the fire fighters waiting for the signal to use the jaws of life to get the driver out of the vehicle if necessary.

"'For now, she has a pulse but it's weak. The screw driver is positioned in such a way it's blocking the carotid artery. If it moves, even a fraction of an inch she could bleed out in seconds," the paramedic standing with the gurney said. "Whoever did this may have wanted her to survive, or, have a slow, painful, agonizing death. Honestly, I am not sure which is worse," he continued. Fiona saw the woman's eyes flutter. She approached the broken window.

"Ma'am, the paramedics are here, they are going to take good care of you. Can you speak?" Fiona asked. "Do you know who did this to you?" She wanted to get whatever information she could before this woman passed out or died. The woman muttered something but Fiona couldn't make out what she was trying to say. It sounded like 'bled dead'. "You are not going to die. Do you hear me? You are going to be just fine." Fiona tried to reassure the stabbed woman. What is it with this killer and sharp objects? She thought to herself. "Whoever did this, were they in the car with you?" Fiona asked leaning her head in the window trying to get closer to be able to hear her. Again, the woman muttered what sounded like 'bled dead', this time the woman had a tear streaming down her face. The visor was pulled down on the driver's side and the mirror was open. Fiona realized the woman could see her reflection with the screw driver sticking out of the side of her neck. The blood slowly dripping down onto her shoulder. She thinks she is going to bleed to death, that is what she was trying to tell Fiona. "You aren't going to bleed to death, you are going to be just fine. Just stay as still as possible until we get you out of here," Fiona said.

"Hey Detective, listen to me, I am going to need you to slowly, and I do mean slowly, slide the back of the driver's seat as far back as you can so I can slide the backboard into place," the lead paramedic yelled to Fiona. It was hard to hear anything with all the emergency response vehicle engines running just feet away.

"You need me to do what?" Fiona said, now in a panic.

"I can't secure her neck with a brace without disturbing the implement. We have to get her on a back board in order to get her out of the car. You need to do this. Find the lever and don't do anything until I tell you to." The paramedic was calm and collected, the exact opposite of how Fiona felt at that precise moment.

Fiona slid her arm into the broken window and extended her right arm down the side of the seat. She was touching the lever. It was an automatic seat adjuster. "OK I have the lever, it's an automatic, how slow do you want me to go?" Fiona asked knowing she held this woman's life in her hands. She thought back to that night with Arthur. She finally accepted that she wasn't responsible for what happened but her heart still told her there might have been a chance she could have avoided such a tragedy. She couldn't deal with watching this woman take her last breath staring up at her.

"On my go, I want you to slowly push the lever. The seat needs to slide back in one fluid motion. Once the seat is far enough down for me to slide the board under her, you can release the lever and then step aside." Fiona took a deep breath.

"Ready? GO!" the paramedic yelled. Fiona pushed down on the lever. She tried to maintain the same amount of pressure, the seat sliding backwards as slow as she could make it.

"That's it, keep steady. OK, you can release the lever now. I should be able to slide the board in," the paramedic instructed. Fiona instantly removed her finger off the button and stepped back, releasing the breath she had been holding in the entire time. Another paramedic moved close to the window and put an oxygen mask over the victim's mouth. Her rubber gloved hand held the victim's wrist.

"Her pulse is picking up with oxygen. We need to get her into the ambulance," the E.M.T yelled to her partner. Fiona watched as they effortlessly slid the patient out of the trunk as if they were moving a delicate piece of furniture and not a human being.

"Where are you taking her?" Fiona yelled.

"We are going to St. Mary's you can ride along with us," the paramedic held the back of the ambulance door open so Fiona could hop in.

Fiona sat and watched the paramedic jump into action. Wires were placed on the victim's chest, machines were beeping. An IV was hooked up. Fiona was amazed how quickly this woman was being cared for. "Miss, my name is Detective Mitchell, did you see who did this to you?" Fiona asked again. The woman's eyes widened as if she wanted to say something. "Can you take the oxygen mask off her?" Fiona asked the paramedic.

"Only for a moment. I know you need to question her but I need to keep her alive until we get to the hospital so make it quick," the paramedic instructed her. Fiona lifted the mask just above the woman's face making sure not to disturb any of the wires or tubes, and certainly not the screwdriver.

"We are two minutes away from the hospital. Just relax. Do you know who did this to you?" Fiona asked for a fourth time. "Bled dead," she muttered again this time clearer but Fiona still couldn't understand what she meant.

"Ma'am you aren't going to bleed to death." Fiona tried to assure her. The woman's eyes widened again. She was looking Fiona in the eye and then to the top of her head. She did this a few times.

"Bled dead," she said again. Fiona was frustrated, her victim wasn't making any sense.

"Detective, I need to put the oxygen back on. We are pulling up to the hospital. I'm sorry." The paramedic said while preparing to move the patient from the ambulance to the emergency room.

"Just one more moment, please?" Fiona begged.

"No! Now move! I need to get her into the hospital." The paramedic yelled at Fiona opening the door to the ambulance. There was a trauma team of nurses and doctor's waiting at the emergency room entrance dressed in disposable yellow surgical gowns.

Fiona followed the hospital team into the E.R. but was told she couldn't advance any further. "She is going straight up to the operating room and you aren't authorized to go past here." One of the nurses yelled to her. The double doors swung open like magic. Fiona felt defeated. She just stood and watched her only living victim roll away. She looked down at her phone and couldn't believe the time. She had been on the scene for over an hour which made her wonder, where the hell was Julian?

Twenty

Olivia Stevens was laying in her hospital bed unaware anyone was in the room with her. She laid with her held tilted to the left. It was the only position she could lay her head where she wasn't in constant pain. The right side of her neck was heavily bandaged. If not for the constant beeping of the medical equipment taking a continuous reading of her vital signs the room would have been silent, but she wasn't alone. In the corner, stood a slim figure, arms crossed over their chest, something sticking out between their fingers. The room was dark, a dim overhead light shone at the top of the bed casting a shadow onto the woman peacefully sleeping. There wasn't much time. When the nurse had come in over an hour ago, the figure hid in the thin closet not wanting to be seen. It was only a matter of time before the same nurse came back in to check on the latest victim. This woman wasn't supposed to have survived. She was supposed to be dead like the others.

The slim figure approached the woman lying in the bed, noticing the victim's eyes beginning to flutter.

"Sshh, everything is ok," the figure said in a soothing voice. "You are going to feel much better in just a moment," the figure continued to speak in a comforting tone. The figure pulled a syringe filled with clear liquid to their mouth, pulled the cap off using their teeth and spit the cap onto the floor. Olivia started to stir again in bed. A small groan released from her mouth. She was in pain. Unable to turn her neck she lay slowly trying to reach for the call button, her eyes still closed.

"There, there, this may burn a bit in your hand but you will be feeling just fine in a minute," the figure said sliding the thin steel needle into the I.V. protruding from her hand. The plunger slowly pushed down forcing the clear liquid into the victim's vein. It wouldn't take long now; in just a few seconds another name would be added to the death list.

The victim started to pant. Gasping for air, her eyes flew open, she was trying to move, feet sliding back and forth at the bottom of the bed but the sheets were tucked in so tightly she didn't have the momentum to release the hospital corners. Sweat started to bead up at her hairline, her left hand swung out trying to reach for whomever was standing on the other side of her causing the call button to fall to the floor. The machines she was hooked up to started to beep, loudly. The light above her head started to flicker in rapid secession. The slim figure removed the syringe from the patient and headed for the door. There were sounds of footsteps fast approaching the room. The figure walked out and down the hall just as the nurses and doctors holding their stethoscopes from bouncing around on their necks ran into the victim's room. The figure made it to the stairwell but tripped and fell down the first flight of stairs. A member of maintenance was walking past the landing just below, he looked up when he heard the commotion.

"You alright up there?" he asked pushing his large garbage barrel in front of him. The figure stuck out a foot showing the maintenance man the sneaker with the laces untied hanging from each side. The figure nodded their head indicating they were fine, bent down and tightly tied the laces of the Nike sneakers.

Twenty-One

Fiona walked into the station infuriated. Julian was nowhere to be found. She called his cell again. "You have reached Detective," the voicemail started to say but Fiona quickly ended the call. Her office phone had a blinking light indicating a new voicemail message. She picked up the receiver standing on her tiptoes watching the front door hoping to see Julian walking in. He was in for a world of hurt when he showed up. First case or not, he knew he needed to stay reachable twenty-four seven. It was the first rule as a homicide detective.

"Hey Fiona, it's Melissa, give me a call when you get in. I heard you were in the field and didn't want to disturb you but I have some news regarding the cell phone your partner dropped off. I don't think you will be happy about it but call me. Call me when you are alone," the message said. Fiona hung up with a concerned look. Why alone? She thought to herself.

She looked around the station and saw several detectives sitting at their desks, their faces looking down at their files, others on their computers filing reports. She thought about the reports she was going to have to type up when she had a moment to catch her breath. The reports alone would amount to another day without sleep. She sat back down, picked up the receiver and dialed the extension for T.A.R.U. No sooner did the phone start to ring when Julian walked up to her desk. Fiona hung up the phone and just glared at him.

"Where the hell have you been?" she spoke in her stern don't mess with me voice. It had been over thirty plus hours since she laid in her bed, she wasn't in the mood for anyone or anything at this point.

"Sorry, I got tied up." Julian replied knowing his excuse wasn't worth the breath it took to utter the words.

"Tied up? I truly hope you are going to tell me, the person who took the lives of two women and put one in the hospital, took you hostage and literally tied you up." She replied, this time her voice was an octave higher. She heard the sound of keys clacking on computers start to slow down. She was drawing attention to herself. She needed to calm down. She didn't want any of her fellow detectives to get the impression she wasn't able to handle the stress of the job.

"I have an errand to run. I will be back in half an hour. Why don't you make yourself useful and call the hospital? Inquire about the condition of the patient that was brought in by ambulance this morning with a screwdriver in her neck. I trust you can do that without getting tied up. Call me when you have the information," she instructed her insufferable prick of a partner. Su Lee was right about that, Julian was insufferable to a fault. Aggravated she grabbed her phone and keys off the desk and walked away leaving Julian with yet another dirty look. She walked a few feet and turned back around.

"You should think about taking a shower and putting on a fresh shirt, you look like shit," she instructed. His appearance was unkempt at best. Something was going on with him. He never looked this bad. Even in the few short days she had known him, she knew enough that he was meticulous about his wardrobe.

She walked into the building adjacent to the station house. This building was much newer and in far better condition. It had air conditioning and heat. Something that was foreign to the police commissioner. There was even a coffee cart with a woman in her early twenties making specialty beverages for all the overworked employees. All she had at the station was an old coffee machine and she had to use a paper towel as a filter half the time.

Fiona was far too tired to take note of how jealous she was. She pressed the up button on the elevator and waited for the doors to open, her eyes heavy with exhaustion. The elevator at the station across the street had been out of order since before she became a detective. Another thing she didn't have the strength to be jealous about. Some people have all the luck she thought to herself as she blew out a breath causing her hair to fall in her face. She needed a shower in the worst way. The idea of hot water on her bare skin felt like a million bucks right about now.

Fiona walked out of the elevator and weaved her way through the aisles of cubicles. She finally got to Melissa's cube.

"Hey girl. I got your message. I figured I would come by before I killed my partner and found myself on the wrong side of the table in the interrogation room," Fiona joked, or at least she wanted to believe she was joking.

"I heard all about your new partner. What was the word Su Lee referred to him as?" Melissa said tapping her manicured nails on the desk.

"Insufferable," Fiona muttered.

"That's it. Insufferable. Su Lee said he's a real piece of work," Melissa said turning in her swivel chair to face Fiona.

"He is certainly on my shit list at the moment. I have been asking myself why I was paired with such a prick. He has a lot to learn and I don't have the patience to train him right now. I am up to my eyeballs in victims." Fiona replied not wanting to gossip about her pain in the ass partner.

"I give you credit; he was here earlier wanting details on the phone that was logged in as evidence. He was talking nonstop wanting whatever information I could give him. By the time he came up for a breath I was ready to strangle him myself. He is sexy as hell as long as he doesn't open his mouth." Melissa went on. "You must have a hunch this phone is going to tell you something because he made me promise that I would contact him before anyone else when I was able to access the photos on the phone." Melissa finished with a roll of her eyes.

"Yeah, he means well. Wants to be helpful but half the time I can't locate him and the other half he is saying the wrong thing at the wrong time. He has a lot to learn," Fiona explained doing exactly what she didn't want to do, gossip.

"I could have saved you the trip and told you this on the phone," Melissa spoke in a quieter tone.

"I needed to get away from the office so the trip was a good excuse as any to leave Julian working on something without me unleashing my temper on him." Fiona explained wanting Melissa to know she wasn't being put out.

"I am waiting on the warrant for the service provider to unlock the phone. I put a priority rush on it, but I am not holding my breath. I made some calls and rumor has it every judge has a full docket today and you know how protective these cell services are." Melissa said with disdain in her tone. Fiona found it comforting that she wasn't the only one frustrated with the roadblocks she was running into.

"Keep me posted and do whatever you have to in order to get that phone unlocked," Fiona demanded, hearing her cell phone chirp in her pocket. She took it out and looked at the message.

"I've got to go; another body has been found. Man, this guy works quick," she said turning on her heels heading through the maze of cubicles to get back to the elevator. She was disappointed she wouldn't have time to treat herself to one of the amazing specialty coffees on her way out of the building. The aroma was making her mouth water.

Twenty-Two

"This is Mitchell" Fiona said parking the car on the curb, two wheels on the curb the other two on the pavement of the no parking zone in front of Spa Newvah. She looked in the window and saw chandeliers with low lights illuminating the front entrance of the chic salon. Why anyone would pay money for someone else to wash their face was more of a mystery to Fiona than the one she was working on. Fiona wasn't into the high-end glamour that was taking the world by storm. She had an unhealthy hatred for the Kardashians and their role in making women believe being shallow and superficial were all the rage. Were women really this stupid? She thought to herself.

"Hey boss lady, I got the skinny on your Vic in the hospital. Name is Olivia Stevens. Doctor says she is going to make a full recovery but it's going to take time. They were able to remove the screwdriver with very little damage. He said something about her blood pressure dropping really low while in surgery and he's concerned about a possible stroke or embolism, I'm not really sure." Julian reported.

"Did you bother to write it down Julian?" Fiona snapped into the phone. He was working her last nerve.

"Yeah, but I am a cop not a doctor. I wrote down everything he said. The best part is that one of her pinky fingers was broken. What's weird is that other than the screwdriver being jammed into the side of her neck there were no other injuries except for the broken finger. No scratches, defensive wounds, nothing." Julian explained sounding more and more like a moron with every passing word.

"Thanks for the update Julian, let the hospital know I will be in to talk with Ms. Stevens after I leave here. Tell them I want a security guard placed outside her door. I don't want anyone in or out of that room other than hospital staff," Fiona explained. She didn't want to tell him she was at yet another crime scene. She needed to handle this one on her own. She needed to focus, not babysit a rookie detective. Julian was distracting her from concentrating on the case. She was now up to three bodies. It was official, she now had a serial killer on her hands.

Su Lee was standing next to a uniformed officer, looking up at him with her neck craned all the way back. Fiona couldn't hear what she was saying, but based on her facial expressions she was in the same mood as the last time they were together. Fiona braced herself for more than just a dead body. Everyone was exhausted and bitchy, herself included. She needed to get whatever information she could and not piss anyone off in the process.

Hey Su Lee, what have you got for me?" Fiona asked keeping a few feet away from the medical examiner. She didn't want her friend to think she was invading her space.

"The victim is Natalie Morales, thirty-one years of age, found in the trunk of her car. Based on temp and lividity I would estimate time of death to be forty-eight hours ago. Unsure about cause of death. No blood found in the car, no evidence of gun shot or stab wounds." Su Lee explained trying to suppress a yawn.

"How was the body found?" Fiona inquired.

"According to Felix, someone parked next to the car this morning, went into the swanky spa, when they returned, they noticed a strange smell. Cops were called and here we are." Su Lee gave her the condensed version, nodded her head and walked back to her van.

"Officer Felix is it?" Fiona asked holding her badge in the air for him to notice. "You were the responding officer to the call about the odor emanating from this vehicle?" Fiona questioned pointing to the gray Mercury Sable encased within yellow crime scene tape.

"Yes Ma'am. I arrived on scene at approximately ten twenty-seven this morning, spoke with the woman who called nine one one. She was right about the odor. It wasn't a pleasant smell. The vehicle door was unlocked. I opened the driver's side door once I confirmed there was no one inside the vehicle. The car looked immaculate. I thought at first someone may have lost a potato in the car. Happened to me about a month ago. Stench was so bad I had to drive with all the windows open and even then it was all I could do to keep from puking. Finally took the car to be detailed and that is when one of the teenagers vacuuming the back seat found the remnants of what used to be a potato. This car is either brand new or had just been cleaned. There isn't a napkin or spare change in the door handle. I released the trunk from inside the car, immediately the odor became more intense. When I looked in the trunk, I saw the body of a late twenty early thirty's woman, face up inside the trunk. I dispatched for additional units and emergency response team. I secured the area and waited for back up." Officer Felix recited not once looking down at his notes.

"Thank you, Officer. Good Work." Fiona patted him on the shoulder with her notepad, thinking how Felix could give her partner lessons on how to handle himself at a crime scene.

Fiona saw the scene was under control. She had the witnesses' statements. There was nothing more that she could do here, she needed to wait for the lab results to come in and Su Lee to conduct the autopsy. Now was as good a time as ever to question Olivia Stevens. She is the only living victim. Fiona looked up at the sky, saying a silent prayer to Arthur to help her figure this out. There had to be something she was missing. There was something about all these women that linked together somehow. Fiona always loved a good mystery, even as a child she would rather watch Dateline than television shows geared towards her own age but this wasn't television. This was real life; women were being brutally murdered and she needed to stop whomever was responsible for these heinous acts. She felt defeated, exhausted and was starting to smell almost as bad as the Mercury Sable. She needed a break, needed to collect her thoughts and take a hot shower.

Twenty-Three

Fiona had no choice; she needed a hot shower and a quick power nap. If the Captain caught a glimpse of her in her present condition, he would have sent her packing. Arthur always taught her to take a moment and get herself together.

"You are no good to the department or the victims if you don't take care of yourself," he would tell her when she was willing to pull three days straight without so much as running a comb through her hair.

The hot shower felt like heaven, but the entire time she knew she should be somewhere else, she felt guilty taking a twenty-minute shower and a forty-five-minute nap on the couch. She did wake refreshed with less fog clouding her brain. She needed to make one more stop and then she would be good to go for at least another twenty-four hours. She had scheduled an interview with the latest victim at the hospital, but right now she was on her way to question someone else.

"Hey Ma! Well look at you, is that new?" Fiona asked wondering where her mother got a bright blue cashmere sweater. She had to admit, the color did look nice on her mother.

"It was a gift sweetheart. Feel it, isn't it soft." Her mother said stretching out her arm so Fiona could feel how elegant the sweater was.

"Yes, it's amazing but who gave it to you?" Fiona questioned.

"I told you it was a gift from your sister. She was here a little while ago. It was so nice to see her again. I can't wait for you two to see each other again. It's been a long time since we have all been together." Her mother explained. Fiona looked puzzled.

"Mom, I don't have a sister. I am your only child. Do you know who I am?" Fiona asked, once again starting with the basics.

"Now Fiona, how many times are you going to ask me. You are my daughter, a detective with the local police force though I don't know why you aren't working for the F.B.I." Bethany winked at her daughter. Clearly her mother was lucid. She didn't want to pressure her with questions but she was concerned.

"Mom, do you know that I am an only child? You never gave me a sibling. It has always just been me and you." Fiona stated calmly. She didn't want to give her mother the indication she was worried.

"Oh, I know that you think you were an only child but your sister didn't grow up with you. She lived far far away. I didn't even know she knew how to find me. I just assumed she died." Bethany replied looking down at her hands folded in her lap with sadness in her eyes.

"Mom, I think you are confused. It's ok. I think you should rest for a bit." Fiona suggested hoping her mother would agree.

"Don't patronize me young lady, I am not confused. Well, maybe I am just a little but it's only because I haven't seen her in years. I was so excited when she showed up the other day. I wasn't even sure it was her but once I took a good look at her, looked into her eyes I knew it was her. I had no doubt in my mind." Bethany snapped at her daughter. She was adamant that her sister was here just a short time ago.

"Ok Mom, whatever you say." Fiona replied with defeat in her voice.

After an episode of the Ellen DeGeneres show Fiona had to leave, Audrey was expecting her at the hospital.

"Mom, I have to go now. I will be back in a couple of days. Please know how much I love you." She kissed her mother on the forehead.

"Oh excuse me, could you please let the maid know I would like another blanket on my bed." Bethany replied looking at Fiona as if she were a stranger. Fiona patted her on the arm.

"Sure thing ma'am." Fiona replied tears forming in her eyes. She was losing her mother little by little. Moment by moment her mother was slowly drifting away from her. It was difficult to see the parent turn into the child. Her mother needed her and there was nothing she could do.

Twenty-Four

"I must warn you detective, this isn't going to be easy. Ms. Stevens has suffered a minor stroke affecting the left side of her body. The right side of her neck is bandaged so mobility is a bit of a problem at this time. I am fine with you questioning her but I must advise if Mrs. Reis feels the patient is becoming agitated, I am going to have to insist you leave and come back when she is in better health," the doctor explained to Fiona.

"Who is Mrs. Reis and why does she need to be in the room when I speak with Ms. Stevens?" Fiona questioned not sure why she, a detective, couldn't be trusted to speak with a victim without a witness.

The doctor rubbed his head holding his pen between his fingers, "I assume no one mentioned to you Ms. Stevens is deaf. She could barely speak words before her attack, now she isn't even able to do much sign language. Mrs. Reis will be there to assist you in translating your questions, since I assume you don't know sign language." He tried to speak with a level of patience, sadly it was coming across as agitation.

"My apologies Doctor, my partner must have failed to mention the victim had a disability. I will do my best to keep my questions brief." Fiona was now just as aggravated as the doctor's tone. How could Julian fail to mention this to her? She wasn't sure what was going on with him but she was going to get to the bottom of it when she returned to the station. Until then, there was a deaf woman who has suffered a stroke that could be the only person to identify her attacker.

"Hello, I am Detective Mitchell you must be Mrs. Reis?" Fiona questioned holding up her badge motioning for the translator to stay seated.

"Yes, please call me Sandi. Mrs. Reis was my mother-in-law. I am not sure how much help I will be to you but I am going to try my best for this poor woman." Sandi said looking over to the bed where a woman was laying looking back at the two of them wondering what was happening.

"Ms. Stevens, I am Detective Mitchell, please let me start off by saying I am truly sorry this has happened to you. I am going to do everything I can to catch the person who committed this vicious act." Fiona said looking over at Sandi when she finished speaking. Sandi nodded and translated everything to Olivia using just her hands. Watching Sandi was like watching art in motion. Her hands moved with a fluidity that was captivating. Olivia looked at Sandi and then to Fiona, making movements with her only good hand and four usable fingers.

"Detective, Olivia has requested we give her a notepad and pen, she thinks she may be able to write simple words." Sandi translated back to Fiona.

"OK, um, here take my notepad and pen. Tell her I will ask yes or no questions and we can go from there." Fiona instructed nodding at Sandi.

"Ms. Stevens, may I call you Olivia?" Fiona started with a simple question. Olivia looked down at the pad and wrote the word 'yes' in what looked to be kindergarten handwriting. Fiona smiled at her victim.

"You were driving the car that we found you in?" Fiona asked. "Olivia pointed to the word yes with her index finger.

"OK, good. Were you alone in the car before you were attacked?" Fiona asked this time looking straight down at the notepad. Olivia used her pen to write the word 'No'. "Someone was in the car with you? Did you know who the person was that was in the car?" Fiona thought this could have been a possible carjacking turned violent. Again, Olivia pointed to the word yes. "Was the person who was in the car with you responsible for your injuries?" Fiona asked, this time making a point to look Olivia in the eye when she spoke and waited for her response. Olivia was a person, not a machine. She needed to be treated like a human being and not an ATM. Olivia pointed to both the yes and no words written on the notepad.

"OK, let's try this another way. Was the person you were in the car with the one who stabbed you with the screwdriver?" Fiona asked knowing she needed to break down her questions into simpler verbiage. Olivia quickly pointed to the word no, lifted up her right hand and waved it back and forth so Fiona could see the metal splint that was wrapped around her pinky finger.

"The person in the car with you only broke your finger?" Fiona asked. Olivia pointed to the word yes. Fiona was starting to get somewhere. "OK so the person in the car with you, they broke your finger. Was this person a man?" Fiona asked starting to feel like she was playing twenty questions. Olivia pointed to the word yes. "Was the person who stabbed you, were they a man as well?" Fiona asked. Olivia pointed to the word no. Fiona looked Olivia in the eye, "No?" Olivia tapped her finger on the word no again. "You mean, a woman stabbed you with the screwdriver?" Fiona needed confirmation she was understanding this correctly. Olivia tapped on the word yes, this time she blew out a small breath. "Did you know this woman?" Fiona was fiddling with her phone at this point wanting to take notes but couldn't with the victim using her notepad.

Sandi was keeping up with the sign language word for word. This wasn't her first time translating. She wasn't frazzled in the slightest. Perhaps this is going to provide the much-needed information Fiona has been waiting for. "Did you know the woman who stabbed you?" Fiona asked trying to type on her iPhone as quickly as she was talking. It wasn't working out as well as Sandi was doing with her hand art. Olivia pointed to the word no.

"Olivia, I know this is going to be difficult but can you describe her at all. Body type? Height? Anything you can think of will be helpful." Fiona asked knowing it would take time for Olivia to write down the words. Olivia looked from Sandi to Fiona and moved her fingers around.

"Detective, she is saying the woman she saw was you." Sandi explained with a confused look on her face.

"Me? Well, yes I was on the scene when the paramedics were transporting you to the hospital Olivia, but did you get a look at the person who attacked you?" Fiona rephrased her question hoping to simplify what she was asking. Olivia looked directly at Fiona and pointed to her. She then touched the top of her head and pointed back at Fiona. "I am sorry Olivia I am not sure I understand what you are trying to tell me."

Fiona was starting to get frustrated. She knew she needed to stay as calm as possible in order to keep Olivia from getting upset. Olivia looked at Sandi, used her only four good fingers and tried to run them through the bottom of her hair, then pointed to Olivia. "I think she is trying to tell you something about her attacker's hair?" Sandi chimed in starting to get excited, like this was some weird game of charades.

"Olivia, the woman who attacked you had long hair?" Fiona asked. Olivia's index finger ran over the word yes on the notepad. Fiona let out a sigh, she thought she was going to hit a dead end but she was able to keep the flow of questioning going. "Did the woman have brown hair?" Fiona asked. This was going to take time but she was the only person with a pulse that could give her any type of useful information. Olivia ran her finger across the word no but pointed to the top of her head and then to Fiona all over again. Something clicked inside of Fiona.

"Are you trying to tell me the woman who attacked you had red hair like mine?" Fiona asked thinking she may have just hit the jackpot. Olivia tapped her finger on the word yes. She too was excited for Fiona to understand what she was struggling to act out. "The woman had red hair, is there anything else you can tell me about her?" Fiona asked.

Sandi didn't bother to raise her hands. "Detective, she isn't going to be able to tell you things that detailed. It will be easier for her to continue with the yes or no questions," Sandi explained.

"Sorry, of course." Fiona apologized. "Olivia, I am going to say some numbers, point to the yes when I get to the age you think your attacker is. Do you understand?" Fiona looked to Sandi hoping she could interpret the point she was trying to make. Olivia bent her three fingers and tried to do her best thumbs up for both Fiona and Sandi.

Twenty-Five

Fiona summoned all parties of her new task force to the conference room. Now that the introductions were finished it was time to get to work.

"As you know, we have three dead bodies and one victim that has been able to give us a few leads but nothing concrete." Fiona said walking over to the white board. "Olivia Stevens stated her attacker was a female with red hair. Similar build and age as myself. In fact, she thought I was the killer. I think she was confused because she was still under some powerful pain killers and may have confused me for her attacker because I was at the scene when they transported her. Further questioning will need to be done once she is up to it. Tavares, you and I will team up for the meeting with Ms. Stevens. Keeping it an all-girls club may make her feel more comfortable," Fiona instructed. Tavares had a noticeable smile on her face. She thought teaming up with Fiona was a marvelous idea. Two women detectives solving what has to be the biggest murder spree this town has seen in over fifty years, had a certain ring to it.

"Detective Correira and Detective Dubois go to the morgue. Stand outside, pace the halls, whatever you have to do, but you aren't to leave until Su Lee gives you the reports on the latest victim. Officer Daniels, I will have T.A.R.U send over the cell phone we found at the second victim's house. They are having trouble unlocking it so if you could try to work whatever voodoo you could on that, it would be extremely helpful." Fiona was handing out orders like she was a drill sergeant. She felt a certain amount of confidence standing in front of her fellow detectives. Whatever fears she had when she walked into the room were slowly starting to dissipate. She knew with the added help she would be able to catch this madman. Or in this case a possible madwoman.

"Um, Detective, what do you want me to do?" Julian asked not sure about his role in all this.

"Why don't you get started on the reports, that is if you can do that without getting tied up." Fiona replied with an attitude. She was still pissed with Julian's performance during this investigation. Whatever was going on with him would have to wait but she was confident she would figure out what he was really up to.

The task force moved around the conference room heading for the door then dispersing in separate directions. Each one of them had their marching orders and Fiona hoped one of them would come back with information that would lead her directly to the killer. Audrey stood behind in the conference room waiting to talk with Fiona.

"When do you think we will be able to question Olivia Stevens again?" Detective Tavares asked eager to get started on her part of the investigation.

"I say we head over to the hospital and see what we can find out. I need to make sure Nurse Reis is going to be available to translate for us." Fiona replied gathering up her notepad and coffee cup.

"Do you think she will be able to tell us anything more? She gave us some info to go on but until forensics comes back with what they find in her vehicle we are at a standstill. The lab said they should have something by this afternoon," Audrey explained. Fiona was impressed with the way she was already familiar with this part of the case. Perhaps teaming up with another female was just what she needed. It would certainly be a change of pace from Julian. Audrey was someone she could talk to without having to explain everything as she spoke.

"Until the lab comes back the only thing we can do is talk to Ms. Stevens. I think she knows more than she told me the last time I was at the hospital."

Twenty-Six

The hospital was busy. A twelve-car pileup occurred less than forty-five minutes ago. There were ambulances everywhere, hospital staff running around trying to prepare for massive trauma when Fiona and Audrey walked in the main entrance. "If the main lobby is this hectic can you imagine what the E.R. must look like?" Fiona mentioned pushing her way through the circular door.

"A real three ring circus is what it must look like. My ex-husband is a surgeon and he hates when there is an accident of this magnitude. He said there were times when he didn't think he could stand up for another minute, and the next thing you know someone was being wheeled into the O.R. that needed him to save their life." Audrey explained with a look of love in her eyes.

"Your ex? You speak very highly of him. Do you mind me asking why he is your ex?" Fiona questioned.

"He found himself playing doctor with one of the on-call nurses. Figures since he was working so much, he would throw in a little play time as well. Cheaters aren't in my wheel house. Good man, awful husband. Now he is single and still working for Beth Israel. I am sure he is making his way through all the female hospital staff," Audrey explained.

"I have to say, you don't seem all that broken up that your marriage fell apart." Fiona replied looking at Audrey with a raised eyebrow.

"It was hard but I too work unorthodox hours as well so part of me couldn't blame him for throwing his hot dog down a hallway, but in the end, I got what I wanted out of the marriage. I got the house and Cooper and Scout." Audrey stated looking down at the elevator floor.

"Are those your children?" Fiona asked wondering who may be babysitting for her while she is working this case.

"Yes, they are. My two four legged children. Australian Shepherds. There is nothing more comforting than walking in the door to two of the most delightful pups. They never judge and are always glad to see me. More than I can say for any human I have encountered," Audrey said laughing. Fiona was glad to know there was another woman in the department just as cynical as her.

At the nurse's station they were informed that Nurse Reis wouldn't be in until three that afternoon. The charge nurse on duty said that Ms. Stevens was doing much better and was due to be discharged in a day or two. Fiona took her cell out, ran her fingers around the keypad of the phone creating a note to remind her to get twenty-four hour surveillance for Ms. Stevens when she left the hospital. She wanted to make sure as the only living victim to these heinous crimes she stayed as safe as possible.

"We have less than thirty minutes and Nurse Reis will be here. We are going to talk to the Security Manager. I want to know why there wasn't a guard outside her room." Audrey took the lead and informed the charge nurse they wanted to see the head of security right away. Fiona was right about this woman. They were going to get along just fine. They thought a lot alike.

Mr. Cote approached the nurse's station. "Hey Jane, I heard someone is looking for me?" he said to the nurse sitting in the chair with a stack of charts piled so high you could barely see the top of the nurse's head.

"Yeah, two detectives right over there want to speak with you. Be careful they seem a little feisty." Jane replied motioning to the small sitting area just to the left of the nurse's station.

"Good Afternoon I am Mr. Cote head of security here at the hospital. What can I do for you Detectives?," he asked unaware of what this matter was all about.

"Yesterday a woman came into the hospital, the victim of an assault. My partner Detective Correira called and instructed someone from your staff to stand guard outside her door. When I arrived to question her yesterday there was no one posted outside, and I can see there isn't one again today. I assume you don't need an engraved invitation to do your job, Mr. Cote is it?" Fiona asked with aggravation in her tone, checking out his silver-plated name tag.

"I am not familiar with anyone calling for added security to a room. Hang on just a moment, let me see what I can find out." Mr. Cote said walking a few steps away from them. Both detectives heard him talk quietly into his radio attached to his left shoulder.

"I am awfully sorry but dispatch doesn't have any record of anyone calling asking for a detail on this room. Any calls coming into the security station are recorded and we don't have any record of your partner calling in such a request. In fact, it has been over a week since we have received a call from anyone from the police department." Mr. Cote explained. "I assume you would like me to assign someone to her room?," he asked wanting to make up for whatever potential danger the patient may be in.

"Yes please, and make sure there is someone outside her room at all times until she is discharged," Fiona demanded. She couldn't wait to hear how Julian must have been tied up and unable to make the call. His head wasn't in the game and she was ready to pull him off the investigation altogether. She couldn't have anyone on her team who wasn't devoted to giving one hundred percent to solving this case.

Nurse Reis found the detectives sitting in the family room, Audrey was on her phone and Fiona was deep in thought. "I am so sorry to keep you waiting. The nurse at the desk said you would like me to translate for you again. I stopped in to see Ms. Stevens and she is eager to speak with you. I am ready whenever you are." When they entered the room, Fiona noticed Olivia had far less bandages on than she did the day before, a good sign that the worst is behind her.

"Hello Olivia, I am glad to see you are feeling better. It must feel like quite a sense of relief to have less bandages around your neck." Fiona said motioning to her neck as a sign of what she was saying.

Olivia looked at Sandi and watched her sign what Fiona has just said. She smiled and nodded, her head pointing to her neck and then motioning like she was wiping sweat off her brow.

"I brought along a friend, this is Detective Audrey Tavares, she is going to sit in while we talk, is that okay?," Fiona questioned. Arthur taught her to always make the victim feel as comfortable as possible, giving them the illusion, they are the one in charge. Olivia smiled and made an exaggerated pucker with her lips and nodded her head.

"The last time we spoke you mentioned the person who stabbed you was a female with red hair just like mine. Is that correct?" Fiona asked wanting to re-establish what they had talked about earlier, confirming she was alert and their first conversation was factual and not pain killer induced. Nurse Reis did her hand motions with the same fluidity as she had before. It was still mesmerizing to watch. Olivia now had the ability to use both hands, one couldn't be raised higher than her chest and the other still had the metal splint on the pinky finger, but she was moving her hands as if she were preforming ballet, graceful even with the restrictions due to her injury.

"Detective, Olivia said the woman who stabbed her looked very much like you. Same body type and age bracket. The woman wore a dress coat. Her eyes were a dark brown, very dark, so dark they looked almost black." Sandi translated. Olivia tapped on the bed rail. She wanted to add something to what she had just signed. Sandi stared at Olivia and put her hand on her mouth, clearly whatever was being said with her hands was shocking to the nurse. Fiona looked at Audrey whose eyes were glued to the victim sitting up in bed. A tear slid slowly down Olivia's face. Whatever Sandi was about to translate wasn't going to be good. Audrey rose from the chair across the room, walked over to the roll away table on the other side of Olivia's bed and handed her a box of tissues. It was emotional to watch someone describe what their attack was like without being able to use their voice, Fiona couldn't even begin to understand what it must have been like for Olivia. Technically she should have died at the scene. It's a miracle she survived.

The nurse sat down in the chair next to Olivia, grabbed her hand and lightly patted it. It was clear the nurse was shocked and needed a moment to collect herself.

"Nurse Reis, please, you need to tell us what Olivia just signed to you." Fiona spoke gently to the nurse, obviously rattled with what she just witnessed.

"Detective, I am sorry. When I agreed to translate, I wasn't prepared for what I could possibly hear. I was just trying to help. Forgive me." Nurse Reis said looking at both Detectives with a tear now streaming down her face. Fiona steeled herself for what was about to be relayed to her.

"Olivia said the man that broke her finger jumped in the car leaving the passenger door wide open while she was at a stop light. He must not have known she was deaf because Olivia could see he was talking she just couldn't make out what he was saying. Olivia can read lips but not as fast as he was talking. She stepped on the gas pedal, running the red light hoping the man would jump from the car. She crashed into the mailbox and the next thing she knew he grabbed her finger, bent it all the way back. She felt the snap. He must have heard it because he smiled and gave the now broken finger a sharp twist." The nurse explained what Olivia told her, the sound of sobs being held back in her voice. "After he broke her finger, he tried to wrap something on it. Ms. Stevens wasn't able to make out what it was but she remembers him trying to put something on her finger. He struggled with whatever it was and finally gave up," Sandi continued.

"What a dick!" were the only words uttered after what felt like an hour of silence. Audrey couldn't help herself. She knew she shouldn't have said anything but her blood was boiling. She hated violence, never understood the reason for it.

"Sadly, I haven't told you everything yet Detective." Sandi said wiping her nose with a crumpled tissue she pulled from her scrub pocket. Olivia was crying at this point, her head looking up at the ceiling above her hospital bed, no doubt asking God why this was happening to her. It was as simple as she was in the wrong place at the wrong time, but the ends certainly didn't justify the means.

"Are you able to continue, Nurse?" Fiona asked, she too was feeling choked up having to watch this woman relive the worst day of her life all over again.

"Olivia signed that a moment after her finger was broken, she saw a shadow reflecting off her driver's side window. The woman smashed the window with her fist that was wrapped in a towel. The man yanked her head by the back of her ponytail, she said it felt like some of her hair was ripped out. The woman said something, but again she couldn't hear, she thinks the woman said "now" but she can't be sure. Just then the man tilted her head towards him, laying it on his chest. The woman then plunged the screwdriver into her neck, waited to see Olivia's reaction and then took off. The man didn't leave the car until after the woman did. He looked at Olivia and she thinks he said "sorry" but again she can't be sure." Nurse Reis was drained by the time she finished talking. Audrey felt a shiver pass through her entire body. She looked at Olivia who was now just staring at the wall.

"I said it before and I will say it again. What a dick!" she muttered. Fiona couldn't believe how this poor woman survived this.

"Olivia, I promise you I am going to do everything I can to catch the bitch that did this to you." Fiona said putting her hand on the victim's foot which was covered by the cheap blanket used at the hospital. "When I arrived on the scene you were lying in the car with the screwdriver still in your neck. What stopped you from trying to pull it out?" Fiona asked, thankful she didn't because she wouldn't be here right now able to tell her story. She definitely would have bled out at the scene. Olivia turned to Sandi and the two of them did their hand dance for a few minutes.

"She said that her father was an E.M.T and he always told her the neck was the worst place to sustain an injury other than the head and chest of course," Sandi relayed.

"Thank you so much for all your help Olivia. I think we have pretty much everything we need. We will be in touch if we have any further questions. If you think of anything please don't hesitate to get in touch with either myself or Detective Tavares."

Fiona and Audrey walked down the hall in silence. They were both still reeling from what they were just told. Audrey was the first to speak.

"We need to find these two assholes. Sorry for the language I just can't stand that the perps who did this to Ms. Stevens are still out there. This woman could be sitting at the local deli having a sandwich scouting for her next victim, blending in like a normal person," Audrey explained.

"This woman could be anyone. It could be her, or her or even her." Fiona stated pointing to the women that were walking down the hospital hallway. An imaginary light bulb gleamed above her head. Fiona grabbed her phone and dialed as quickly as her finger could move. She was walking at a brisk pace, Audrey had to speed walk just to keep up with her.

"Daniels, run my face through the data base and let me know if you get any hits. Yes, my face. Use all my information, height, weight, hair, eye color. Call me back if you get a hit on anything. Tavares and I are on our way back to the station." Fiona shouted into the phone as if she were ordering a coffee through the drive-up window.

"Man, I didn't even think of that. Olivia said the woman who attacked her looked a lot like you. They say everyone has a twin in this world." Audrey stated thinking they were finally on to something.

Twenty-Seven

Fiona started the Crown Vic, fastened her seat belt and took a deep breath. If this woman was responsible for all the murders, this would be the first ever female serial killer this town had ever encountered. She glanced over to Audrey who was staring out the window.

"Something on your mind Audrey?" Fiona asked. She needed to make sure her new side kick was able to handle the living victims, not just the dead ones. She thought about Arthur.

He always said, "The dead don't talk; it's our job to do the talking for them."

"No, I just can't get the picture of what happened to Olivia out of my mind. Do we know where her vehicle is?" Audrey asked taking her phone out and dialing as fast as Fiona did just a few minutes ago.

Fiona maneuvered the car through traffic wanting to get back to the station and find out if Detective Daniels was able to make any progress. There had to be any number of women who shared the same features as her. The captain would want to know about this. If somehow this got leaked to the press it would cause severe speculation that perhaps one of his detectives was moonlighting as a killer. The last thing she wanted was to have her Captain blindsided. She started to dial the Captain when she noticed an incoming call from Daniels. "What'cha got for me Daniels?" Fiona said eager to hear what he had to say.

"Are you sitting down?" Daniels asked before saying anything else. "I am driving, I am two minutes away from the station. What's up?" she asked, anticipation causing her voice to quiver.

"Get in here, I got something you are going to want to see with your own eyes." Daniels said disconnecting the call. Daniels leaned back in his office chair, there it was in his monitor, a mug shot that was a dead ringer for Detective Fiona Mitchell staring right back at him.

"This has to be a mistake." Detective Daniels said to himself swiveling back and forth in the office chair. Though the photo wasn't an exact replica of Fiona it was a ninety-nine percent match according to VICAP. They say everyone has a doppelganger but this was uncanny. The similarities in their appearance were spot on. Daniels tried to access as much information as he could on this Fiona look-alike. The records were sealed, only a juvenile record was listed. He would have to gain access from the courts in Alaska in order to get all the information he could on the person staring back at him.

Twenty-Eight

Fiona couldn't believe what she was looking at. The mug shot was uncanny. It looked just like her. "Did you pull her file?" she asked Detective Daniels.

"Already requested the records from Alaska Department of Corrections," Daniels replied.

"Zayna Onyx Morgan and I have the same date of birth. What are the chances?" Fiona asked with a puzzled look on her face. She couldn't help but see various similarities between her and the face looking up at her from the paper she was holding in her hand.

"Do we know anything, anything at all about this woman?" Fiona asked, her hands now shaking causing the paper to crinkle.

"Morgan has no record here. It seems like the only trouble she got into was when she was a juvenile. It's going to take time for the Alaska D.O.C. to unseal those records for us, but I took the liberty of having one of my sources do a little digging. She found out your look-alike spent quite some time in a mental hospital in Alaska. She wasn't able to get specifics but from what I can tell from their website, the North Star Hospital in Anchorage specializes in mentally insane juveniles, and not just your average run of the mill mentally disturbed, but the real crazies." Daniels relayed the information to Fiona.

"Your source is a "She"? Anything you care to elaborate on?" Fiona asked with a raised eyebrow.

"Come now Fiona, I am sure Arthur taught you a good detective never kisses and tells." Daniels replied trying to lighten the mood in the squad room.

"Fiona? Fiona? Hello?" Audrey stood next to Fiona but she didn't even acknowledge Audrey standing there. Fiona wasn't paying attention to anything;

all she could do was stare at the picture she held in front of her. Audrey tapped her on the shoulder causing Fiona to pull herself out of her trance.

"What is it Audrey?" Fiona asked exasperated.

"I have something from the lab. The hairs found in the bathtub drain at Amelia Leach's house match those found in the car of Olivia Stevens. The techs went through Ms. Stevens entire car and only found one hair that didn't belong to the victim. They are an exact match. Both hairs found are those of a natural red head," Audrey explained.

"Same as me." Fiona stated rattled.

"Fiona, listen to me." Audrey said turning Fiona by the shoulders so they were facing each other.

"I know this is a lot to absorb, this Morgan woman looking a lot like you and all but she isn't you. I don't know who this woman is or what her connection is to these murders but it's not you." Audrey tried to explain.

"There is more to this photo than you know Audrey. I am not sure how to explain it. I am not sure I even understand it myself." Fiona mentioned as she grabbed her jacket off the back of her chair.

"I have to go. I will be back later. Daniels, call me the minute you have those files from Alaska." Fiona said as she walked toward the exit of the station house.

Twenty-Nine

"Is Marjorie in today?" Fiona questioned the nurse.

"Yes, she is, may I tell her who is inquiring?" The nurse wearing a Mickey Mouse scrub top asked.

"Please tell her Detective Mitchell is here and I have some questions regarding the woman who came to visit my mother the other day," Fiona replied.

"Okay, please wait over there and I will get her for you. She isn't on this floor today so it could be a few minutes before she comes up." The nurse replied with a friendly tone. Fiona was in a mood that was far from friendly at this point. Fiona wasn't positive but she had a feeling her mother was in danger. She put her hand in her coat pocket and felt the folded paper containing the photograph of Zayna Onyx Morgan. She took a deep breath and silently prayed this was the one time her gut instincts were wrong.

After almost a half hour Fiona stood up to stretch her legs. These chairs were far from inviting. She was jittery but this time it wasn't from too much coffee. Fiona started to pace and saw Marjorie walking towards her. "Oh Marjorie, thank God you are here," Fiona said before the woman was even within ear shot of hearing her.

"Hi Detective Mitchell, Nurse Mello said you needed to speak with me. Is everything all right? You don't look so good. Perhaps you should sit down." Marjorie stared at Fiona's pale face.

"I am glad you were able to get away and speak with me. I won't take up too much of your time and please, call me Fiona," she told the nurse sitting back down in the uncomfortable chair.

"Okay Fiona, what is it that I can do for you? Is there something wrong with your mother?" Marjorie asked with tension in her voice.

"I am not sure, which is why I'm here. When I was here yesterday my mother mentioned that woman came to see her again. She referred to her as my sister. As I told you on the phone, I am an only child as is my mother. It's impossible for me to have a sibling. I don't even have any cousins or family other than my mother." Fiona started to explain. "When you called me, you mentioned the woman who came to see my mother looked a lot like me. Do you remember that?" Fiona questioned the nurse as if their phone conversation took place months ago and not less than two days prior.

"Well yes Fiona, I do remember. She had the same red hair as you. Same body type and bone structure. At first, I thought it was you, thought perhaps you and your mom had a quarrel and you left to keep from escalating the argument, but when I got in the room you were there a moment later unaware of why your mother was so upset." Marjorie explained still unsure of what this was all about.

"Is this the woman who came to visit my mother?" Fiona asked unfolding the crinkled paper from her pocket. Marjorie held the photo in her hand, looking from the paper to Fiona and then the paper again.

"Yes, this is the woman. She is younger in this picture but I am almost certain this is the same woman that came in to see her." Marjorie stated confirming Fiona's fears.

This woman was a criminal, possibly clinically insane, what on earth did she want with my mother? Fiona asked herself. "Marjorie, please if this woman comes in again, I need you to call me A.S.A.P. Please don't mention that I asked about her. I don't want to upset my mother or this woman, whoever she is," Fiona ordered the nurse.

"I am not always on this floor but when I am, I can keep an eye out. Do you want me to mention this to the other nurses so they are aware as well?" Marjorie inquired with a raised eyebrow, knowing there was more to this than the Detective was telling her.

"I am going to talk to the charge nurse and try to get you assigned to my mother for the next few days. I trust you with my mother, you have always been very kind to her and I know that she likes you. Are you okay with that?" Fiona asked with sympathy in her eyes.

"I guess so, is she in any danger?" Marjorie asked not sure what to make of the request. She didn't want to get involved in anything dangerous and based on the Detective's tone, the hair on the back of her neck was starting to tingle.

"Honestly, I don't know. All I know is I have a serial killer on the loose, a living victim who claims the woman who attacked her looked very much like me and now this woman whom my mother claims to be my sister is visiting her." Fiona stated. "I don't want to scare you but you are the only person that I trust with my mother. She is comfortable with you. If you are caring for her you could keep an ear to the ground and let me know if she mentions this woman again. Please, I wouldn't ask if I weren't concerned about my mother. The last thing I want is for you or my mother to be in any danger. I am going to arrange for an undercover officer to be here to keep an eye out for anything out of the ordinary. All I need you to do is let me know if my mother mentions anything to you about this woman or if the woman returns." Fiona begged. She was starting to shake, letting her nerves get the best of her which right now was not what she needed.

"Fine, I will talk to the charge nurse and let her know she will be hearing from you. If she agrees to change my shifts, I will take care of your mother. She is a wonderful lady and very little trouble. To be honest, it will be nice to take a break from the more difficult patients for a few days. Some give me a run for my money and let's face it, I am not getting any younger." Marjorie stated agreeing with apprehension in her tone.

Fiona worked out all the details with the nursing home and the undercover officer. She could rest easy that at least her mom was protected from whomever this madwoman may be. She had no evidence, Zayna Onyx Morgan was responsible for the attacks but she wasn't going to take any chances when it came to her mother's safety.

Thirty

"This is Mitchell!" Fiona yelled into the phone. She was on her way to visit Su Lee when Detective Daniels called.

"Mitchell, I was able to get Alaska D.O.C. to send the juvie records for Morgan. She had quite the childhood. She has a rap sheet almost as long as some of the lifers we have sitting on death row. All done before she hit puberty."

"Just give me the highlights will you Daniels," Fiona snapped. The time for a preamble had come and gone.

"Looks as if what finally put her away was the charge of attempted murder on her last foster mother. According to the police report, Morgan claimed the foster mother was aware her husband was sexually abusing her and didn't do anything about it. Morgan ran away returning five days later with a knife, snuck through her old bedroom window, made her way to the kitchen and stabbed her foster mother eleven times while the victim was standing at the stove making dinner." Daniels reported.

"Damn, eleven times, and the woman survived?" Fiona asked, trying to envision a child over powering a grown woman. She had to have some rage inside her to take on a woman twice her size.

"Barely, she spent over two weeks in the hospital. Had to have her spleen removed, then turned septic. She is lucky to be alive. Morgan had just turned twelve. Judge decided to err on the side of caution and put her in North Star until she turned twenty-one. She had numerous brushes with the law but this must have been the one to seal her fate. Ironically, she was released on her twenty first birthday. What a way to celebrate being legal to do just about anything in this country, by being released from doing something illegal." Fiona wasn't sure how to process all this new found information. There was still nothing linking her to the crimes but something inside Fiona told her this was her girl. Now all she had to do was find her and prove it.

"Assemble the task force. I want everyone in the conference room in thirty minutes." Fiona ordered into the phone.

Fiona walked through the door like a woman on fire. She was trying to keep herself together but it was a struggle. In addition to searching for a killer she was now panicked about her mother's safety. "Glad to see we are all here." Fiona glanced around the room.

"Where is Correira?" Fiona asked now seriously pissed off. How dare he miss a briefing when there were details that needed to be sorted through.

"No one knows. We have all tried his cell phone but it goes directly to voice mail." Detective Dubois answered. "I tried to ping his cell but it must be turned off. I can't get a read on him at all," Detective Daniels stated.

Fiona was infuriated but she didn't have time to dwell on Julian being tardy. She would have to deal with him later.

"As you know, Detective Tavares and I spoke with Olivia Stevens and she confirmed that her attacker was in fact a female but with a male counterpart. He was responsible for the broken finger. She also stated the male attacker tried to place something around her finger at the time of the incident but failed to do so." Fiona started off with the details she herself obtained. The other detectives would have their turn at the podium.

"Tavares, why don't you take it from there." Fiona gave the podium to her new partner, at least she hoped so, the Captain would make the final decision.

"The car was impounded and the C.S.U. department found one red hair on the driver side door jamb. This hair is an exact match to the hairs found in the drain of our second victim Amelia Leach. There is no way these two attacks aren't connected. A blue string the length of a lollipop stick was found on the passenger seat cushion. This could be what Olivia Stevens mentioned. Our first victim, Felicity Osborn had a finger lodged in her throat. A blue string was wrapped around the finger and tied in a small bow. Again, we have a connection between Olivia Stevens and Felicity Osborn. The only one we don't have a connection to is the woman who was found in the trunk in the parking lot of the spa. It looks as though we are still waiting on the M.E. report for her and C.S.U. is still processing her vehicle." Audrey walked back to her seat waiting for the next round of information to be presented.

Fiona was still trying to link her look-alike to these murders but nothing tangible has been found. Detective Daniels was the next to take the floor.

"As you all know Ms. Stevens stated her attacker looked a lot like Detective Mitchell. Per her instructions I ran her stats through facial recognition and came up with one hit. Zayna Onyx Morgan. D.O.B. is eleven nineteen eighty-eight, single, only a juvenile criminal record, did nine plus years in a psychiatric hospital for the clinically insane, released in twenty oh nine. No information after that date. Other than the physical features of Morgan we are unable to link her to the murders." Detective Daniels finished his report.

"I guess I will go next." Detective Dubois raised from his chair but didn't bother walking to the front of the room. There weren't enough people to consider this a crowd so he stood right where he sat knowing no one would have an issue hearing him. "I have spoken with Su Lee and she is doing the best she can to get us up to the minute information as it becomes available. I spoke with the wife of Mr. Souza, the man who found Amelia Leach on his front lawn. She was shocked that all of this happened but did tell me Amelia worked for a law firm specializing in open adoptions. They became friends when the Souzas were having a difficult time conceiving and wanted information on adoption in case they decided to head in that direction. According to Mrs. Souza Amelia was dating a man but wasn't sure of his name. I retrieved the deceased's phone from Melissa in T.A.R.U and gave it to Detective Daniels. He is currently trying to hack into the phone since we haven't heard back from the judge regarding the warrant for the cell company. Su Lee reported the blood found on the two stuffed crocodiles was that of the victim. The interesting fact, there was a blue string tied in a bow attached to each of their tails. Again, connecting the murderer to this victim as well." Dubois finished his report and sat down.

"Thank you all for your hard work in this investigation but sadly we aren't done yet. We know the same person killed two women and maimed a third. Our fourth victim is still awaiting a connection to the previous three. I am going to assume all four are connected somehow. What we need is tangible evidence against Morgan in order to obtain a warrant for her arrest. Until then we need to keep digging. Dubois, I want anything and everything you can find about Zayna Onyx Morgan. I want to know where she was born, grew up. I want to know it all. If she so much as had a sleepover with a friend from fifth grade I want to know who it was with and how to contact them. Daniels, work on getting into Leach's phone. If she knew of Zayna there could be a phone number, photo, text, something to help us find her."

Fiona handed out instruction like a drill sergeant. Everyone started to leave the room with their own set of marching orders. "Let's meet back here in a couple hours and re-group, hopefully we will have something more to go on." Fiona added loudly so the team walking through the doorway could hear her.

"What do you want me to do Mitchell?" Audrey asked.

"Get me the home address of Julian, we are going to pay him a little visit and find out what he has been doing that is prohibiting him from helping with this investigation."

"On it Boss, I will get the address and meet you in the parking garage." Audrey said making a saluting motion with her right hand. Both Fiona and Audrey started to laugh.

"Thanks, I needed that laugh especially since I am heading in to brief the Captain on the status of our investigation." Fiona said, the laughter no longer lingering in the air having been replaced with apprehension.

Thirty-One

Audrey was already in the car with her seat belt on before Fiona even got to the parking garage.

"Got the address?" Fiona asked putting on her seat belt. She wasn't used to anyone but her driving, it was something she would have to just deal with.

"Yup, he lives in a really nice area. He doesn't have an apartment number; he has a Suite. La de da," Audrey replied with a raised eyebrow.

"I am sure it's courtesy of his father, the Governor. No way he can afford a place like that on his salary," Fiona replied.

"His father is the Governor? No wonder he thinks he can come and go as he pleases around here. His shield is politically protected." Audrey replied her comment dripping with sarcasm.

"Well look at you getting all aggravated about what I hope to be my former partner." The statement threw her for a loop. Whenever Fiona thought about her "former partner" she always envisioned Arthur, but she realized that had all changed now. Julian Correira was her partner but she was going to do everything in her power to have him reassigned. Regardless if he politically protected or not, she wasn't going to let him or anyone else drag her down.

"I am aggravated Fiona; I can't believe you aren't. It's hard enough for women to get their shield these days, not to mention the male detectives don't take us seriously with their old boys club routine, and here Julian walks in with everything probably handed to him. It just grinds my gears. I bust my ass every day and have earned my stripes but because his dear old dad is connected, we get pushed aside for promotions all because we aren't men." Audrey took a deep breath now that her rant was over.

Fiona knew she had a point. Even in today's world it's still difficult for a female to be taken seriously when only a decade ago there were even less females in the homicide unit. Fiona was from the school of hard knocks. Everything she had in life was achieved through hard work either by herself or her mother. She knew the price her mother paid to make sure Fiona had everything she needed in life even if it meant working various jobs so Fiona could have extra. "I hear ya Audrey. It's irritating but I am a firm believer that hard work will get you noticed not whatever title your father may have written alongside his name." Fiona stated trying to calm Audrey, who was behind the wheel screaming at other cars in traffic. Clearly, she had a temper. Fiona was actually impressed.

Thirty-Two

The elevator door opened directly into the entrance way of Julian's suite. The moment the doors slid open they were met with a cold blast of air. It was colder inside than it was outside. November was generally a cold month. What was Julian thinking still having his central air on full blast? The view of his suite appeared to be that of a penthouse. How connected was his father? This place had to cost upwards of three grand a month. Fiona tried to think of anyone she knew who could afford such a lavish lifestyle. Certainly not her. She was blessed with a house without the weight of a monthly mortgage thanks to her mother's years of hard work. Bethany wanted to make sure when her daughter inherited the house it was debt free. True, Fiona put a lot of money into fixing it, trying to make it her own space but it didn't compare to the palace she just walked into.

Fiona quickly reached to her side; she moved the length of her jacket behind her to unclip her weapon. She glanced at Audrey who was mimicking her every move.

"You heard it too?" Audrey whispered. Fiona nodded her head, pointing with her finger indicating they were going to proceed into the living room. With both their guns drawn they slowly made their way several feet forward from the foyer to the actual suite. At first glance, Fiona could tell a struggle had taken place. Neither were wearing gloves, touching anything was off limits. Both detectives surveyed the area. The lamp was broken, two wine glasses were shattered on the floor spilling red wine on what had to be a thousand-dollar oriental rug. Fiona knew how meticulous Julian was with just about every aspect of his life. There is no way he would have just left this mess on the floor. The living room, dining room and kitchen were designed with an open floor plan. Three of the six dining chairs were overturned, one of the legs looked to have been broken off. Fiona squatted next to the chair with the broken leg, without touching the jagged wooded edge she could see traces of blood. The blood hadn't been there for very long, it was barely starting to get tacky. The kitchen didn't seem to be disturbed other than the wine bottle on the counter next to the corkscrew. Whatever started calmly in the kitchen took a dangerous turn as they made their way into the living room. Audrey turned in all directions to ensure there was no one left in the room and motioned to Fiona to continue down the hall. Fiona nodded in agreement. This was no longer two colleagues checking in on another, this was now a crime scene. Several scenarios flooded Fiona's mind. Perhaps Julian was drunk from too much wine, stumbled into the chairs knocking them over, breaking one of the legs. If he cut himself on the broken chair that would definitely explain the blood. There were too many variations to run through, they needed to find Julian and figure out what happened.

A low guttural sound came from the far end of the massive hallway. The hallway was lightly furnished with only a bench and wall table causing the sound to echo off the walls. Audrey turned slightly to look back at Fiona. She was nervous, as was her partner. With no idea what they were about to uncover they both proceeded as carefully as possible making sure to clear and secure each room before moving on the next. Each time one of them closed a door to indicate the room as been checked the sound got louder. They were unable to locate the source with each passing room but they knew they were walking towards it. They were almost to the last bedroom. Only two more doorways to check. Fiona wanted to run ahead and find the source of the noise but she knew better. She had to follow procedure. She couldn't risk it, having no idea if someone was still lurking in the house, leaving Audrey at risk to secure them alone. Her heart was pounding out of her chest. She was afraid of what she was going to find at the end of the hall. Whoever this killer was they were all searching for, they were creative when it came to their murders. Anything was possible at this point.

The only room left was the door at the end of the hall. As both women approached the guttural sound now turned into a moan, it sounded like something whimpering. The door to the room wasn't wide open as the others were. This door was closed only halfway. There were no lights on in the room, no small lamp to illuminate a shadow of any kind. Fiona could see the blackout shades were drawn causing the room to appear even darker than it actually was. At the doorway Fiona grabbed Audrey's arm and whispered, "On my count we go in, you go to the left and I will head straight. What or Who is in that room is injured. What we are hearing is the sound of pain. Once the room is cleared call for back up and an ambulance." Fiona took a deep breath, never realizing all this time she had been panting.

Audrey nodded her head and gave Fiona a thumbs up. She too inhaled deeply, instead of panting she was holding her breath. With wide eyes she looked at Audrey, held up one finger, then two, then three. Both women burst through the partially opened doorway. As instructed Audrey went to the left and yelled "clear". A few seconds later Fiona did the same. There was no one in the room with them, whomever was in this room had exited using the window, the scent of their perfume and the metallic scent of blood still lingering in the air.

The weather outside was dry and windy. The blackout shades were swaying back and forth, the room was freezing, there was no mistaking the window was either left open or broken, Fiona wasn't sure which. Audrey used her elbow to flip on the light switch, that's when they both saw it. Blood, not a drop or a trail. The walls, rug, and lamp were all covered in blood. Some areas had splattered blood, others had small puddles. Bloody hand prints covered the walls like a kindergartners finger painting. Shivers instantly ran down Fiona's spine. How could she let this happen? Again. The full-length mirrors that made up the doors of the walk-in closet were splattered with blood. It looked like red confetti was stuck to the mirror. In the center of the mirror written in blood were the words, "How could you forget?"

It took a moment for Audrey to gain her composure. She felt like she was in her early twenties again, waking up hung over after a rave party. The walls were covered in spray paint, similar to the blood markings covering every inch of this room. "Dispatch this is Detective Tavares, roll additional units to the address of Detective Julian Correira. I also need emergency response units and C.S.U. We have an officer missing, possible abduction, I repeat an officer is missing." Audrey slid her gun into its holster her hands shaking the entire time. Less than an hour ago she was sitting in the car with Fiona ranting about female detectives not being treated as equals yet here she was rattled to her very core, doing nothing to prove her point. They both froze exactly where they were standing glaring at each other. They both heard the sound again. It sounded close, really close. They both looked around but no one else was in the room. Where could it be coming from? Fiona slid the mirrored closet door open not wanting to disturb the bloody handwritten message. When she cleared the room, she opened the closet doors and made sure it was empty but she had to look again. Audrey walked around the entire perimeter of the bed and came up empty. The only thing she found was one bloody footprint. The imprint was perfect. Luckily there was just enough blood to create a perfect impression, the blood having congealed just enough to prevent from smearing. She took a picture of it with her phone, there was something about this impression that was familiar to her but she wasn't sure what it was. She knew when she had a moment to clear her head it would come to her.

"What the hell happened in here?" Audrey asked Fiona who was staring at the lettering on the mirror.

"How could you forget?" Fiona whispered over and over. What was she supposed to remember?

"Fiona?" Audrey yelled, startling Fiona out of her thoughts.

"Sorry, what?" she asked. "I called it in, additional units are on their way along with C.S.U. and an ambulance, though there doesn't seem to be anyone here for them to treat".

As if on cue they both heard the whimpering, this time it sounded like it was coming from the window. Audrey walked over to the window, slowly used her phone to move the blackout shade forward and peeked outside. Directly out the window, on the enclosed balcony was Julian, his hands and feet were tied behind his back with duct tape across his mouth. He had dried blood all over his face and neck. His shirt was ripped, his shorts wet with what she hoped was perspiration but even if it wasn't, she couldn't blame him, she felt like she could pee her pants at any moment.

"Oh my God he must be freezing." Audrey exclaimed. On instinct she reached for the duvet on the bed to wrap him in. Before her hand connected with the fabric Fiona grabbed her arm.

"Detective Tavares, you can't touch that. This isn't our friend's home anymore. This is a crime scene and Julian is the victim. We need to follow all procedures to the letter. We can't make any mistakes. Whoever did this, just signed their death warrant. Every officer in the state will be gunning for them.

"Mitchell, we can't just leave him out there like that. He is freezing, it's barely fifty degrees outside, who knows how long he has been out there." Audrey pleaded with her superior to help him.

"Get an ETA on the ambo, find out where those additional units are. I am going out on the balcony to assess the situation. Remember don't touch anything!" Fiona ordered her partner.

Fiona pulled her arm into the sleeve of her jacket, and pulled the shade up, getting a clear-cut view of Julian curled up on the balcony shivering from what she assumed was both cold and fear. The window was wide open so whoever did this didn't gain access to the suite using the window as their entry point. Could Julian have opened the door for them?

"Hey Julian, it's Fiona. We have help on the way, try to stay calm. Julian tried to look at her but based on the way he was positioned he couldn't see her; he could only hear the sound of her voice. He let out another whimper. She took large steps closer to him not wanting to disturb whatever evidence may be out there. "I am going to rip the tape off; it's not going to hurt. Well maybe a little, not any worse than when I get my eyebrows waxed." Fiona was trying to keep the atmosphere light. Julian was a metro sexual; he was aware of the pain involved with waxing. Even with the tape across his mouth she could see he was trying to smile. Fiona couldn't help but feel responsible for this. She should have kept an eye on him, kept him at her side at all times but she was so caught up with gaining the respect of her peers that she put him in harm's way. With the tip of her thumb and index finger she gently grabbed the edge of the tape and without warning she ripped the tape off with one fluid motion. Julia let out a groan, moving his mouth up and down. Fiona was certain it was a relief for him even if his mouth was stinging. The sides of his lips were pink and getting darker by the second. Fiona held onto the edge of the tape waiting for C.S.U. to arrive. She heard the sirens getting closer, they would be here within minutes.

Thirty-Three

Julian laid on the gurney, both his arms covered in gauze bandages. His head hurt like hell. It felt as if his head was trapped in a vice grip. He reached for the call button, he needed something for the pain, but it slid off the bed falling to the floor. He extended his arm and made a low pitch moan as he did so. Fire shot through his entire right side.

The commotion caused Fiona to wake up. She had fallen asleep in the chair in his emergency bay. They hadn't even admitted him to a room yet. So much for special treatment for law enforcement. The curtain to his bay was drawn and the light turned off. She was relieved when the doctor informed her that Julian was going to be okay, that he looked worse than he actually was. Luckily, he had no internal injuries, nothing life threatening. Fiona was grateful for Julian's prognosis, losing another partner was not in her wheel house. She was determined to do right by this one, even if she hadn't thus far.

"Hey buddy, how are you feeling? You gave me quite a scare." Fiona said quietly not wanting to excite him.

"I feel like I went a couple rounds with Mike Tyson, did I at least win?" he asked feeling embarrassed that he was lying in the hospital bed.

"Afraid not. The doctor says that you are going to be just fine. No internal damage. Said you look worse than you feel but right now I must say, you aren't looking too good." Fiona said glancing down at the floor. She felt guilty, she felt it was her fault this happened to him and because of that she couldn't look him in the eye.

"Is there anything I can get you, water maybe?" Fiona looked in his direction. He could have asked for a Mercedes Benz and she would try to figure out a way to get him one, she was feeling that guilty.

"Water would be great as long as I can wash it down with a couple Vicodins. My entire body hurts, I am not even sure which part hurts more. My limbs, abdomen or my head." Julian replied reaching up to touch the lump on this forehead.

"Let me go find the doctor." Fiona said as she pulled the curtain wide open.

Julian laid in the hospital bed wondering how he was going to tell Fiona the truth. He had been carrying this news around and he was getting tired. He knew he was a dead man if he talked but keeping his mouth shut would only cause more harm. How many more deaths can he carry on his shoulders? This nightmare has to stop. She told him it was only going to be one body. One dead person in return for his silence, that was the deal. She promised. He kept his end of the bargain but she didn't. Now was the time to return the favor, now he would go back on their deal. His family would hate him, he would lose his shield. If he kept quiet no one would ever know, but he would know and that wasn't something he could carry with him for the rest of his life. His confession would change everything. With one simple statement people's lives would change in a New York minute.

The nurse walked into his bay holding a small silver plastic square in her hand and a cup of water. She scanned the bar code on his hospital bracelet, then the square pack. "Here you go Mr. Correira, you should be feeling a little more comfortable in about fifteen minutes." Fiona, only a few steps away, corrected the nurse.

"Nurse, it's actually Detective Correira." The nurse looked at her patient.

"Mr. is fine Nurse, really," Julian replied. This was not the time he needed his partner to refer to him as a detective. In a couple days when the dust settles and he is stripped of his badge it won't matter what people call him. He knows what he will be, a prisoner, just like he is now only the world will know what he has done.

"I am going to let you get some rest. I spoke to your father and he is going to have someone come get you when you are released. The nurse said you don't need to be admitted but you need to take it easy for a few days. Your father said you will be staying with him and your mother since your place is now a crime scene. I will stop by tomorrow to talk to you about what happened. No sense in doing it now, you have taken your pain meds and will be drowsy soon. I know this was the Forget Me Not killer. A message was left on your closet door. We are patrolling the area but I doubt we will find anything out tonight. Get some rest and I will see you soon." Fiona said patting him on the arm.

"Sounds good, I am exhausted and need some sleep. I will tell you everything tomorrow." Julian replied, his eyes already getting heavy.

"Good night Julian, see you later." Fiona said sliding the curtain to the side just enough to get out of the bay.

"See you later alligator," Julian mumbled.

"Wait, what did you just say?" Fiona asked turning around. She looked back at Julian who was already asleep. Did she imagine it? No, she knew what she heard.

Thirty-Four

After a night in her own bed Fiona felt only slightly refreshed. She didn't sleep much but being snuggled under the covers was comforting. The feel of her own sheets, the smell of her shampoo on her pillows made her feel like she was in a safe place. She crawled out of bed and shook the crumbs off her chest, the only evidence she had eaten an entire sleeve of Oreos. She had a sense someone was watching her ever since she left the hospital. She needed to talk to Julian. She needed to know what happened in his suite. She couldn't get what he said out of her mind. "See you later Alligator." The same thing her mother used to say to her every day when she left for school. She was certain her mother would still say it now, if she could remember.

Fiona saw her mother two days ago but it felt like an eternity. She needed to spend more time with her. Who knew when the day would come when her mother wouldn't remember her at all? She pushed the thought from her mind. Fiona didn't like to think such things. When that time came, she wasn't sure how she was going to handle it. Once her mother was no longer in her right mind, she would be alone. Left alone to deal with life all by herself. The mere thought of it took her breath away.

Less than two years ago, she had everything anyone could ever want in life. She had a mother who loved her, her dream job as a detective and a partner who she considered to be more of a father than a partner. Now, her father figure was gone, her mom barely remembers her own name and her dream job was turning into a nightmare.

"This is Mitchell." Fiona said into her cell phone.

"Hi Fiona, this is Marjorie. You wanted me to call you if that woman came back." Marjorie's voice didn't sound as upbeat as it did the last time she called.

"Yes, are you telling me she visited my mother again?" Fiona asked, this time she wasn't attempting to hide the nervousness in her voice.

"Actually, she is here now. She arrived about ten minutes ago. I would have called sooner but she was asking me questions about your mother's care. I called as soon as I was able to leave your mother's room." Marjorie explained with the same nervousness in her voice as Fiona.

"Thank you for calling Marjorie. I need you to go back into her room and listen to what they are talking about. Do not leave her alone with my mother. I am on my way." Fiona instructed the nurse.

"What am I supposed to do in there?" Marjorie asked, confused as to what was actually being asked of her.

"I don't care, think of something. I need to know what this woman wants with my mother. Please Marjorie, my mother is all I have left in this world. I wouldn't ask if I wasn't worried about her. I will be there in twenty minutes." Fiona was now yelling into the phone as she bent down to put on her boots.

"Okay, I will do what I can but please get here as quickly as possible. I am a nurse not a police officer." Marjorie said as she hung up. Fiona felt awful, she was putting Marjorie in what could be potential danger but what other choice did she have, this was her mother they were talking about. It was Fiona's responsibility to protect her.

Fiona managed to get to the nursing home in under twenty minutes, using her police light and breaking every traffic law known to man but she was desperate. Slightly out of breath she walked into her mother's room and looked around. The only people in the room were her mother, and Marjorie.

"Hi Mom, how are you today?" she bent down and kissed her mother on the cheek. She caught a whiff of her mother, the perfume she was wearing wasn't her normal Shalamar. "Well don't you smell pretty today. Is that a new scent you are wearing?" Fiona asked glancing at Marjorie.

"Yes, you brought it to me earlier Fiona don't you remember?" her mother replied. "You also brought me those flowers because the other ones were dying," her mother continued pointing towards the windowsill. Fiona felt her body run cold.

Fiona walked out of her mother's room. She was confused throughout their entire visit which was heartbreaking to Fiona. No daughter could love a mother more than Fiona loved Bethany. She wasn't even sure her mother knew how much Fiona loved her. Many nights Fiona laid awake staring at the ceiling wishing she could make her mother better. She consulted various specialists, tried all kinds of medication, even tried an herbal homeopathic approach but nothing seemed to work. This disease was taking over her mind and there was nothing anyone could do to stop it.

"When I got back into her room the woman was sitting with her on the edge of the bed. Your mother explained how much she missed seeing her and it wasn't her fault that she stopped writing to her. Your mother told her it was all your fault because you stuck her in this place."

Fiona took a step back, not wanting to hear what Marjorie was saying. "You know I had no choice but to put her in here. She was starting to become a danger to herself. It was the hardest decision of my life. I agonized for weeks whether or not to place her here." Fiona explained starting to cry. Her emotions had taken over and she was too exhausted to try fighting them back.

"Oh honey, I know you did. It's never easy when a child needs to make the decisions you were faced with. Trust me, we have seen it before. No one wants to place their loved one here but sometimes there is no other choice to be made. It doesn't mean you don't love her. It means you love her enough to do whatever needs to be done to protect her." Marjorie tried to reassure her.

"She is my mother and I have failed to protect her. I placed her here so she wouldn't harm herself and now there is someone visiting her, who knows if she is pretending to be me and I can't do anything about it. What kind of daughter am I? I am a detective for Christ's sake!" Fiona cried.

"Did you know your mother was writing someone? She said she had been writing her for years. Your mother called her Zee. I am assuming this was some sort of pet name she had for her." Marjorie was trying not to dump everything that transpired between her mother and the mystery woman fearing Fiona would get upset.

"Marjorie, my mother called her Zee? Like the letter?" Fiona asked transitioning from daughter to detective.

"I suppose it could be the letter, I just assumed it was a nickname or something. I didn't really give it much thought. I was trying to hear everything they were saying without looking as if I were eavesdropping."

"I know, I can't thank you enough for what you did. Marjorie, does she really look like me?" Fiona asked not really wanting to know the truth but needed to.

"Fiona, I am afraid she looks exactly like you. Today she had her hair in a bun but it is red just like yours. She has a small flower tattoo on the side of her neck just under her right ear. In fact, it looks similar to the flowers she has been bringing your mother, the ones she placed on the windowsill." Marjorie was just as nervous as Fiona was. She put herself in the crosshairs and was still feeling the effects of it. Her nerves were shot, she knew there was more to this woman than Fiona was letting on.

"Marjorie, thank you so much for looking after my mother. I have to go but please stay with her until you hear from me." A light bulb went off in Fiona's mind and she wanted to get to the station and review the murders with her task force.

"One more thing, the entire time she was sitting with your mother she was fiddling with a blue string in her hand. She would wrap it around her finger then unravel it. She did it over and over again, like she had a nervous tick or something. It was awfully peculiar." Marjorie added.

"A string, that is odd." Fiona responded leaving Marjorie where she was standing, Fiona heading for the door.

Thirty-Five

Julian was right where the housekeeper said he would be. Laying on the couch with his arms propped up on pillows, watching the DIY channel. This house was enormous compared to his suite but it was to be expected. The Governor wasn't going to live in a shack.

"Hey Fiona, I am glad you are here. I was beginning to think you were so disappointed in me you weren't going to bother coming to see me." Julian greeted her with sad eyes.

"I am glad to see you are feeling better but what is with all the pillows? Neither of your arms were broken." Fiona questioned his position on the couch.

"That would be my mother, she has been coddling me since I got here last night. She thinks I am going to collapse any minute. She has always been the overprotective type. I finally sent her to the store for ginger ale just so I could get a moment alone so your timing is perfect. Please, sit down." Julian reached for the remote control and turned the t.v. off.

"I need to go over the events of yesterday. Your suite is in shambles, clearly you were attacked and I need to know everything you can remember." Fiona stated. She took out her phone and placed in on the table in front of her. She wasn't going to bother taking notes, this time she was going to record their conversation.

"There is a lot I have to tell you and some of it you aren't going to like. I have spoken with my father and he doesn't want me talking to you without a lawyer but at this point it doesn't really matter," Julian said sitting up on the couch. His bandages were bloody. He had some deep lacerations on this neck and arms but like before they looked worse than they actually were.

"A lawyer, Julian you were attacked. You are the victim, there is no need for you to have a lawyer. You didn't do anything wrong." Fiona reassured him.

"If only that were true. Fiona I am so sorry for what I am about to tell you. I didn't have a choice. She was blackmailing me. I wanted to come to you right away but I knew if I did, I would lose my badge, not to mention this isn't the first thing I wanted to tell my new partner. I thought I could handle it but then things started to get out of control and I didn't know what to do. I don't have to worry about losing my badge, I have to worry about being sent to jail. Fiona I am in a lot of trouble here." Julian said, the tone of his voice indicated he was getting things off his chest.

"Julian, what are you talking about?" Fiona asked, pointing to the cell phone reminding him their conversation was being recorded.

"It's fine, I have to tell you what happened and deal with the consequences. I have no choice. It's going to ruin my life and my father's but I see no other alternative." Julian explained not worrying about their conversation being recorded. He had bigger problems to contend with.

"Julian, perhaps you should have a lawyer present. If you are going to incriminate yourself you should consult with an attorney or at least your union rep." Fiona advised.

"There is no time for that. What I have to tell you is urgent. You need to understand I didn't have a choice. I had to choose between Felicity Osborne and my father." Julian tried to stand up but the soreness in his abdomen proved to be too painful.

"Do you know something about the Osborne murder?" Fiona asked.

"I know who killed her, and all the others." Julian confessed. His shoulders slumped as he said the words. He had been holding it all in for almost a month and was finally relieved that it was all going to come out. His conscience would be clear even if his future wasn't.

"What are you saying Julian? You know who the killer is or you know the killer?" Fiona needed to know if he was trying to solve these murders or if he was protecting the killer.

"I wouldn't say I know the killer but yeah, I know who killed all three women and almost killed the Stevens woman." Julian said adjusting his position on the couch because he knew they were going to be there for a while.

"You need to back up. Tell me everything from the beginning. Are you sure you don't want to have a lawyer present? I am recording your statement so I need to ask." Fiona advised him once more. Julian nodded his head.

"This is Fiona Mitchell badge number three one five four one. Present is Detective Julian Correira making a statement regarding the Forget Me Not Killer. Julian for the record please state your name." Fiona formally instructed him.

"My name is Julian Jean Corriera."

"Ok Julian, you can begin whenever you are ready." Fiona leaned back on the couch unaware of what she was about to hear.

Thirty-Six

"The day I met her the weather was really hot. I was going for a run, but wished I had opted for the beach. After about two miles I felt someone was following me. I turned and there she was just a hundred yards or so away from me. I thought she was flirting with me at first but I learned later that I couldn't have been more wrong. I kept running my normal route but when I got back home, she was standing in front of the lobby door. She must have known all along where I lived and had a car parked not far from where I saw her running because there was no way she could have beat me here, not to brag but I run an eight-minute mile. There aren't a lot of women who can keep up with me."

"She asked if she could speak with me about a case she was reporting on for the local paper. I had just come back from Miami a couple weeks before and had barely gotten unpacked. I figured what could it hurt right? I could get to know her and hear about whatever case she was working on. Nothing wrong with having a journalist owing you a favor, right?"

"After we had a bottle of water, she wanted to use my laptop. She wanted to show me what she was working on. When she turned the screen so I could take a look, I saw a video of my father and Aunt Tessa in a not so, how do I put this delicately, let's just say they weren't behaving the way normal siblings should behave. She threatened to leak the video to the media if I didn't do what she asked. I was scared Fiona. You know who my father is. A scandal like this would ruin him. She was blackmailing me and I had to do what she asked. I had no choice. I told her I was a detective and what she was doing was illegal, but she already knew who I was. She said my occupation was going to come in handy with what she had planned." Julian stopped to sip his coffee. He was already looking pale and exhausted.

"From what you have told me so far Julian whomever this woman is, she was the one breaking the law, along with your father and your Aunt. Are you sure it was the two of them in the video, people can do some pretty impressive things with editing these days?" Fiona questioned.

"I confronted my father and he finally confessed. His and my Aunt's relationship dates as far back as their childhood. I am disgusted with my father's antics but he is still my father. He is the Governor of this state. I had to protect my family's reputation. Don't you understand when this gets out it's going to ruin all of us!" Julian yelled. His anxiety level was on the rise but he needed to tell the rest of this sordid tale.

"She told me the price for keeping her silence regarding my family's secret was to use my father's influence to get assigned as your partner. I thought it was as simple as that at first. I spoke with my father and he made it happen. She said once she was done with what she needed to do she would leave town and give me the copy of the video before she left. I didn't think that was that big of a price to pay to keep my family's name from being dragged through the mud, but then Felicity Osborne was murdered."

"I didn't make the connection until she called me right after we left the jewelers. She told me to sway you from the investigation which is why when we were questioning Felicity's father, I made the accusation he was having an affair with his daughter. I knew all along that he wasn't but I was hoping it was a lead you would follow up on and by the time you hit a dead end she would be long gone. She called again and said another woman was going to be murdered because someone still hadn't learned their lesson. I thought she was talking about me. I thought because I didn't screw up the Osborne investigation enough another woman was going to die because of it. I hoped she was just toying with me, wanting to see me shake in my boots, but then we found Amelia Leach."

"I was the first one on the scene because she called me and told me where to find the present she left. I was horrified when I got there. I thought for certain this woman was dead because of me. In a way Amelia Leach died because I didn't have a set of balls to come to you or the Captain right away, but I don't think she was trying to punish me. After the Leach murder I told her I was done, she could release the tape and my family would have to do whatever damage control they could, but I was done being part of her brutal plan. She told me if I helped with one more thing, she would give me the tape and leave me be. I would have been free. I could have washed my hands of all this and put in my resignation stating I didn't have the stomach for the Homicide Unit."

"What I didn't know was that I would be helping her attack Olivia Stevens. She told me to jump into her car and put the string around her finger and she would do the rest. At the last second, she told me to hold her head to my chest, she didn't' say why, I thought she just wanted to scare her. I was so nervous I couldn't get the string on Olivia's finger. When I held her head to my chest and saw her coming at her neck with the screwdriver I panicked. I whispered to the woman that I was sorry and I ran. I ran like a little girl. I let a woman almost die because I am a coward." Julian paused again for another sip of coffee.

"If it's any consolation Olivia Stevens is going to make a full recovery." Fiona said not wanting to change the subject. She knew there was more information coming her way. How much more she didn't know but she wanted to drain Julian of everything that was in his head. He owed her that much. If he had come to her from the very beginning it could have saved the lives of all of these women. Fiona agreed, Julian was a coward. He was just as responsible for these murders as if he was the one wielding the weapon. Even with daddy paying a high-priced lawyer Julian's fate was sealed. He would be lucky to get out on parole before he was seventy. Fiona was fighting back the urge to slap cuffs on him right now but she didn't want him to abide by having the right to remain silent. She was going to refrain from unleashing her temper and wait until the time was right.

"I thought since I told her I didn't care if she leaked the tape or not, she would have been done with me. She would leave town and I would be free of her. I started to worry how I would live with these bodies on my conscience but I just wanted her out of my life. I would figure out a way to deal with everything else. She told me Olivia Stevens was supposed to die. She was pissed that I let her live. Can you believe that she was blaming me? I reminded her that I had full knowledge of all of her crimes and if she wanted to leak the tape to go ahead and I would have her arrested and it would be a serial killer's word against a well-respected Governor." Julian stopped speaking abruptly. Fiona thought he was just pausing to gather his thoughts but after a few moments she thought maybe he was finished.

"Is that everything Julian?" Fiona asked still unsure of who the killer is. He said he knew who killed these women and so far, she hadn't heard a name. "Yes, I am done. I have nothing more to say. This interview is over." Julian said with a firm tone in his voice.

Fiona was pissed. Why would he confess to being an accomplice to three murders and one attempted murder yet never divulge who the actual murderer was. Frustrated Fiona stopped the recording on her cell phone and placed it in her pocket. "Julian, based on what you have confessed I have no choice but to place you under arrest. I need you to stand up and put your hands behind your back." Fiona said sliding the handcuffs across her fingers, feeling the cold steel.

"Wait, Fiona there is more I have to tell you. I think it's best if you don't record it because it involves you."

Thirty-Seven

Audrey was waiting for Fiona in the conference room. She knew something was up when she wasn't answering her texts. Audrey paced the room waiting with nervous anticipation. She had so much to tell her and wasn't sure how Fiona would take the news. Fiona stormed into the room, tossing a stack of files onto the desk and removed her jacket before noticing Audrey pacing in the corner.

"Where are the others?" Fiona snapped.

"I sent them to get sandwiches, I figured we would be here for a while and would need sustenance. I need to talk to you and want us to be alone when I tell you what I found." Audrey explained. The idea of them being alone was starting to feel like a bad idea.

"Make it quick because I have plenty to go over with all of you." Fiona said sending a text to the rest of the team to get back here A.S.A.P.

"Listen Fiona, you need to hear me out but I think you need to sit down." Audrey snapped. This was not the time for her to get a jelly belly. "OK, let's hear it." Fiona said taking a seat at the table.

"The lab results came back from Olivia Steven's car. Two different hairs were recovered that didn't belong to the victim." Audrey started, she could hear the quiver in her voice even though she was trying to maintain a sense of calm.

"Okay, did you run it through VICAP and see if you got a hit?" Fiona asked.

"Fiona, I know you are all worked up about this case, I know I am too but I need you to let me tell you everything before you start asking questions. Please just listen." Audrey had a pleading look in her eyes.

"Okay okay, let's just get on with it." Fiona was eager to get on with her theory but until the team arrived, there wasn't anything she could do so she decided to hear what Audrey had to say.

"I ran the hairs through the database and got two exact matches. One for Julian and one for you." Audrey began again. This sounded so much better when she rehearsed in the mirror in the locker room.

"Julian? He wasn't even at the Steven's crime scene." Fiona mentioned but Audrey put her hand up indicating Fiona needed to practice a bit of patience.

"At first, I thought the hair that matched yours was simply cross contamination since you were at the scene and leaned into the car when the paramedics asked you to move the seat back, but then Su Lee called. It seems the hairs that were taken from the drain at Amelia Leach's bathtub came back as a match for both the victim and you again. Su Lee didn't want to believe it. She ran the test four times. Each time it was a perfect match for you. Before you say anything please, just let me finish. When Su Lee was examining the body of Amelia Leach there were skin cells found under her fingernails. Again, they matched your D.N.A. perfectly."

"Fiona I know there is a reasonable explanation for this but honestly I am freaking out here." Audrey finished, taking a deep breath and waiting for Fiona to say something. "Please tell me what I am thinking isn't the truth. Please tell me you aren't The Forget Me Not Killer." Audrey asked aware that she could be making the biggest mistake of her career

"Audrey, listen to me, you have this all wrong. I am not the killer but I know who is. I talked to Julian. He explained everything about what happened in his suite. He is being blackmailed by the killer. It seems his father is involved in some shady business and the killer is using it against Julian." Fiona didn't go into detail about the Governor's shady business, even though she gave it some serious thought.

Arthur told her to always trust her gut, from the beginning she knew there was something off about Julian but couldn't figure it out. She should have looked at him a little more closely. The answers to all her questions regarding Felicity Osborne's murder were literally staring her in the face every time she looked at Julian.

"What? Julian was involved with the killer?" Audrey asked with a raised eyebrow. "Where is that insufferable prick. I am going to show him how involved I am in this now. He has a lot of nerve using his badge to hide three homicides." Audrey was outraged. Less than twenty-four hours ago she was ranting about how men have it so much easier than women on the police force, Julian's involvement in these murders might be enough to send her over the edge.

"He is in custody, I just left him in central booking with his daddy's lawyer. His suit probably cost more than my car but it doesn't matter. I have his full confession on tape. He isn't trying to deny his involvement. He wants to cooperate fully." Fiona explained but couldn't help but wish she had a chance to unleash some of her rage on him for a few minutes. Because of him people were dead, one woman was maimed.

"The boys are on their way back, tell me what else you found out." Fiona told Audrey. Her partner looked apprehensive, not sure if she could trust Fiona. Audrey had all the evidence she needed to put Fiona away for life. She could close this case and possibly get promoted to Sergeant. The idea of solving these cases would be the biggest fuck you to the fellas on the force. True it would be a gratifying moment but looking at Fiona made her think differently. She stood up, looked Fiona straight in the eye and knew there was no way she was being led down a rabbit hole. Fiona wasn't a killer; Audrey could see it in her face. She was worried about something. Something she wasn't telling her.

"Alright Fiona, I'll show you mine if you show me yours. Deal?" Audrey said holding her hand out to shake Fiona's. Fiona took her hand and placed it firmly in Audrey's. "Deal."

Audrey walked over to the white board against the wall. "Once I got the lab results from Su Lee I spent some time trying to figure out how you did it. I mean, not you but who ever was framing you. Oh this is coming out all wrong. Look, I know you didn't kill these women but I just can't understand how someone could plant all this evidence matching your D.N.A without you knowing." Audrey was frustrated. She felt awful explaining to Fiona that she spent the day trying to prove her partner, the only woman detective on the force she looked up to wasn't a cold-blooded killer.

"I understand Audrey, really I do. Perhaps it would be easier if I go first, that way you won't feel so bad trying to pin these killings on me." Fiona replied to Audrey with a wink.

"Always trying to lighten the mood even when you could be facing the death penalty. I just hope you know what you are doing. Su Lee and I are the only ones who know about your DNA being linked to these murders but it won't take long for the rumor mill to start buzzing, so whatever you have let's hear it." Audrey said knowing this was the eleventh hour.

"Julian explained a lot more about the killer after I turned off the recording. He didn't want what he was about to tell me to go on record since it involved me. It seems when he was first approached by this woman and shown the evidence of what his father was involved in, he wasn't aware of who I was. The day we first met Felicity Osborne's body had just washed ashore. He was nervous but I just assumed it was because he was new to the department, this was his first homicide case, and we never had a chance to meet formally. I mean, what a way to meet your new partner, two strangers standing over a dead woman. Turns out the woman who was blackmailing Julian was me. Not me me but a replica of me." Fiona knew what she was saying was utterly confusing. There was no easy way to explain it. She exhaled deeply and just made the statement as if she were reading it off a cue card.

"Evidently, I have a twin." Fiona could feel her body run cold as she said the words. When she listened to the rest of what Julian had to say after she turned off the recorder, she didn't utter a word. Even when he was done speaking the only time she opened her mouth was to read him his Miranda rights. Until this very moment the words 'I have a twin' never passed her lips. Fiona wasn't even sure she fully processed it all. All her life it had only been her and her mom yet that entire time, thirty-three years, there was someone out there with her exact face, exact hair color, exactly the same fingerprints, the same DNA and she never knew it. She had a sister. A sister who was a killer.

"I'm sorry you have a what now?" Audrey said, confusion written all over her face.

"I have a twin, a sister. I didn't believe it at first but after I arrested Julian and left him to rot in the holding cell, I did some digging. I went to the hospital; a friend of mine is a nurse who had helped me out on a few cases I worked over the years. She had medical records pull my mother's chart when I was born from the archives.

"My mother was very young when she had me. She was a teenager. She didn't know she was having twins. No one ever told her. She had only one ultra sound during her pregnancy because she didn't have any real insurance. She was living on government assistance and the insurance didn't cover additional ultra sounds unless it was a medical necessity. Because my mother was healthy there wasn't a need for further ultrasounds."

"Until the day she went into labor she thought she was only having one baby. After she gave birth, the second baby, my sister, was very small, and had a laundry list of things that were medically wrong with her. When I read the chart I couldn't pronounce half of the medical terms let alone know what they meant, but the records indicated that her mortality rate was very low. My mother signed her maternal rights away and only kept me. Somehow the baby survived and was adopted by the Morgan family. They relocated to Alaska shortly after the adoption was final." Fiona looked exhausted.

Audrey stood with wide eyes, her hand over her mouth, in complete disbelief. "I don't know if this question is appropriate, but does your mother know about any of this? Have you talked to her about it?" Audrey asked quietly, her voice barely above a whisper.

"As you know my mother has Alzheimer's and is confused most of the time. The night of Amelia Leach's murder my mother had an episode at the nursing home. It seems my sister paid her a visit. My mother was insistent she was there. She was upset that I didn't get a chance to meet her. She said it had been so long since she had seen her. It was all very erratic. A nurse called me later that evening and informed me she too had seen the woman my mother was talking about. She mentioned the woman had red hair but that was all she could remember of the woman at the time. I asked her to keep an eye on my mother."

"My sister was there again today but by the time I got to the nursing home she had already left. Marjorie the nurse, said she looked exactly like me. Only after Julian confessed the whole truth did I start to believe the woman visiting my mother and the Forget Me Not killer were one and the same. I just need to prove it." Fiona finished explaining and sat down in one of the chairs at the end of the table. She looked like a beat dog, this was a lot for anyone to comprehend, finding out you have a sister you never knew existed and identifying a serial killer was bound to take the wind out of anyone's sails.

"Luckily I think I have all the proof you are going to need to put your sister away for the rest of her life." Audrey said. She looked at Fiona after realizing what she had just said. "Oh, Fiona I am sorry. I can't imagine how hard this must be for you. Are you ok?" Audrey asked.

"Yeah, I won't lie this is shocking news but just because this woman and I share the same DNA may make us sisters, biologically, but we aren't family, she is a stranger to me. A killer. I am worried about my mother. I have no idea how much of my sister she remembers. She has never mentioned her to me, not ever." Fiona explained knowing Audrey didn't mean anything by her comment to lock her sister up and throw away the key.

"Do you think your mother is in danger?" Audrey asked.

"I'm not sure, this woman came here for a reason. She could have killed anywhere. She chose here because of my mother, or me. Maybe even both. I have around the clock security at the nursing home. No one goes in or out without their say so. For now at least, she has protection but I won't rest easy until this woman is caught." Fiona said with a fire in her eyes.

"All right then let's get to work." Audrey said clapping her hands walking back to the white board.

"Your sister had to come here to target either you or your mother. It's the only plausible explanation. The question is what does she want? She can't possibly think you are going to welcome her into your family with open arms after she killed three women. It's clear she must be suffering from some mental health issues but based on how calculated these murders were I highly doubt she lacks simple common sense." Audrey commented while writing everything they knew about the murders on the white board.

As she listed the victim's names and D.O.B. with a black dry erase marker she froze. She couldn't believe what she was seeing. She turned to Fiona who was now reviewing the files she brought in with her. Audrey stepped away from the board to take another look. She wanted to make sure her eyes weren't playing tricks on her. All of the victims have the same date of birth. There was no way this was a coincidence. What were the chances? As she stood staring at the board she noticed something else. Something just as odd. "Um, Fiona she isn't done," Audrey stated.

"What do you mean, she isn't done?" Fiona asked barely paying attention to what was being said, she was diving through her files looking for something she must have missed the first time around. Audrey kicked Fiona's chair snapping her out of her trance.

"Look at the board will you!" Audrey yelled frustrated that Fiona wasn't paying attention to her.

"Sorry, I know I missed something and I need to find it. She had to have left something more than a wake of dead bodies. If she were after me or my mother there would be some type of clue, message, something. She wanted me to find out who she was, she just didn't count on Julian confessing."

"Well hold on to your britches because I think I may have found your needle in a haystack." Audrey said finally happy Fiona was listening to her.

"I was writing everything on the board so the boys would be able to study it when they get back. All the victims have the same date of birth and if that isn't disturbing enough take a look at all the names of the victims, notice anything peculiar?" Audrey asked.

Fiona stared at the white board as if she were trying to solve the logic puzzle in the Sunday newspaper. "I'm sorry Audrey what am I supposed to be seeing?" Fiona snapped frustrated with herself. She couldn't seem to get her head in the game. Her mother's safety, Julian's involvement not to mention the fact that she had a sister were flying though her head at the speed of light. She couldn't seem to make sense of anything at the moment, her head was in a fog. Audrey walked up to the white board and erased the first letter of each of the victim's name. She then rewrote the letters with a red dry erase marker leaving the rest of the letters in black.

"Do you see it now?" Audrey asked.

"Holy shit, nice work Tavares."

"She isn't done. She has one more on her list. It makes sense. We need to find her before someone with a name starting with the letter "I" is murdered." Both detectives stood staring at the board when the rest of the task force walked in.

"Well well, what are you ladies just standing around for, I thought you said there was a lot to discuss?" Detective Daniels joked dropping a paper bag filled with sandwiches onto the table. Fiona turned to the group of men making their way into the office.

"If you don't want Audrey to send you to the morgue with a tag on your toe I would cut the sarcastic comments and get down to business." Fiona quipped.

"Sorry boss lady, just trying to lighten the mood. I could feel the tension as I put my hand on the doorknob. What have you got for us?" He asked with his proverbial hat in hand.

"As you know, Zayna Onyx Morgan and I share many similar qualities. Based on a confidential informant we have learned that Zayna and I are sisters. I never knew about her obviously, I have no time to explain it all but while you fellas were out doing only God knows what Audrey here put it all together. Take a look at the board. She didn't want to broadcast Julian's involvement in all of this right now. Fiona felt it was best to keep his identity a secret until she had Zayna in custody. She didn't want anything made public, it could send Zayna into hiding and right now what Fiona needed was to draw her out.

"We believe that Fiona, her mother or both are being targeted by the killer. Regardless of their biological relationship with Morgan there is evidence that Zayna was responsible for all of these killings and we don't think she is done. We believe there is at least one more possible victim. If you take a look at the board, all the victims were born on the same day." Audrey started to recite all the evidence she had collected. She wasn't going to tell the team she was actually building a case against her partner. Thankfully, Fiona saved her that embarrassment.

"Not to interrupt you Detective Tavares but the victims aren't the only ones to share a birthday. Both the killer and I share the same date of birth as the victims." Fiona motioned for Audrey to continue with her presentation of the evidence. Audrey regained her focus, and continued.

"We have hair, and skin cells all confirming the DNA belongs to a woman by the name of Zayna Oxnyx Morgan. Just before the rest of you arrived here, Fiona and I took a look at the list of the victims. The first letter of each of the victims is a letter in Fiona's name. Felicity, Olivia, Amelia and Natalie. The only letter missing is the letter I. It's fair to assume Zayna has one more victim." Audrey looked around the room and was pleased to see the same confused face she was wearing less than one hour ago.

Detective Daniels was the first to speak. "So, Mitchell, you and the killer are actually sisters. Identical sisters based on the DNA that was recovered at the crime scene in addition to the photo we pulled from the database. How do we know that you aren't the actual killer and using the sister angle to pin it on her?"

Fiona couldn't blame him for being suspicious. This information was difficult to explain. "I understand your skepticism but I swear to you I had nothing to do with these murders other than trying to hunt down their killer. Up until this morning I thought I was an only child. I haven't even spoken with my mother about any of this yet. As most of you know my mother isn't well and her condition may prevent her from comprehending any of this. Audrey and I trust our informant. We have no reason to believe that he or she would be

steering us in the wrong direction. Please fellas try to have a little faith in me."
Fiona knew this wasn't going to be an easy sell but these boys knew her, they
knew Arthur, they couldn't possibly think she could kill people the way these
women were gruesomely murdered.

"I believe you Mitchell, what do we know about this Morgan woman?"
Detective Dubious chimed in, the sound of his straw sucking up the last of his
soda set Fiona's teeth on edge but at least she had two people in her corner,
hopefully the rest would follow suit just as quickly.

"According to her medical records I obtained from the hospital she
spent three hundred and forty-one days in the NICU. The reports show even
though she survived there could possibly have been some form of brain damage
but at the time it was too early to diagnose." Fiona explained.

"Another reason to suspect she is targeting both you and your mother
Mitchell, the medical report from Su Lee shows Amelia Leach sustained three
hundred and forty-one stab wounds. Most were superficial, the deep gash to her
abdomen was determined to be the fatal wound but regardless, she has a stab
wound for each day Morgan was in the NICU. This can't be a coincidence."
Audrey said interrupting Fiona.

"This may also explain the reason for the two stuffed animals that were
left on the victim's stomach. She wanted you to know there were two of you.
Clever girl." Detective Daniels stated.

"If she wasn't a cold-blooded killer, I would consider her very creative
with the way she staged the bodies." Dubious added.

"We can all sit around praising her bizarre imagination once she is
behind bars, until then don't bother opening your mouth if you don't have
anything substantial to add to this case." Fiona was beginning to lose her
patience.

"All of these women were born on your birthday and they all have a
letter in your name, there has to be another connection to you and her that we

haven't figured out yet. We need to start from the beginning and review every detail, even the smallest. She is telling us something and we need to figure it out," Daniel said.

"This is why I became a detective. I have always enjoyed solving puzzles." Audrey mumbled as she grabbed a victim file and started her review.

The conference table was a mess, there were wrappers laying open filled with half eaten sandwiches, crumbs were scattered all over the table, and in the crease of some of the files. Detective Daniels had a dab of mustard smeared into his shirt. The room was quiet. Everyone was nose deep in their case files. Each eager to come up with something before the other did. The unspoken competition was making each detective work a little harder.

"I think I got something," Dubois shouted. Fiona, Audrey and Daniels leaned back in their chairs waiting to hear. Each of them, stretching their backs, thankful for the change in position. "Mitchell, you are working on the Stevens' file. What was her occupation?" Fiona flipped the pages hearing the crinkle of several sheets being flipped over the top of the manila folder.

"Olivia Stevens, date of birth, November twenty second eighty-three, currently employed as a liaison for child and family services specializing in special needs adoptions.

Why what have you got?" Fiona asked.

"I have the Natalie Morales' file, the victim that was found in the trunk of her car in a parking lot. Date of birth the same as yours, she was a social worker." Dubios stated.

"Holy shit!" Audrey exclaimed. "I have the Leach file, same date of birth, Amelia was a lawyer whose main focus was open adoption, securing the birth mothers' right to have contact with her child." Audrey couldn't believe it.

They all turned to Daniels. He was working with the Felicity Osborne file. "Same birth info which we already established; she was adopted blah blah blah he said as he skimmed the file. Ok here we go, she was adopted through the Making Forever Families Foundation." He sat back in his seat; fingers laced behind his head. "Am I the only one seeing a theme here?" he questioned figuring this was the perfect time to bring back the sarcasm.

"It's more than a theme," Audrey replied holding her finger up, she had something to add to this round table discussion. "Amelia Leach handled several adoptions for that same agency." The room fell silent, it was clear all four detectives were rattled. It took a lot of research and planning to pull off killings of this magnitude. These weren't crimes of passion, these were well thought out premeditated murders.

"She has been trying to tell me who she was this whole time. She wanted me to figure out she was related to me." Fiona rubbed her forehead. She was starting to get a migraine.

"But why kill? Why not just introduce herself to you?" Audrey asked. There had to be more to this than what they were seeing.

"Audrey, grab your coat we need to go." Fiona yelled grabbing her jacket from the back of her chair tipping it over. "Shit!" Fiona said. Daniels touched her shoulder.

"Hey take it easy. We will get her. Just take a breath. I know this is a lot for you to process but you need to set aside your emotions. You need to handle this like you would any other case. Arthur would be pissed if he saw you right now." Fiona knew he was right. She needed to pull it together.

"Audrey, grab the photo of Morgan and let's go. Boys, keep digging we will be back in about an hour." Fiona said zipping her coat, heading for the door.

Thirty-Eight

Fiona parked the car and took a look around the parking lot. "The last time Julian and I were here this place was a ghost town, now it looks more like New Year's Eve at the nut house. We may be able to get what we came for." Fiona reached down the side of her seat and grabbed the picture of Zayna. When she glanced at it all she saw was her own reflection, as if she were looking in a mirror. "It's so odd, this woman looks exactly like me yet is the exact opposite of me. I'm a cop, she is a criminal."

"I guess we know what side of the nature vs nurture debate she falls on. You both may have been born by the same woman but her upbringing had to be completely different than yours, that may be the only way to explain why she turned out to be a homicidal serial killer and you became a cop. You two are the definition of good versus evil." Fiona could always count on Audrey to point out the obvious.

The bar was packed, not a single seat available. Fiona made her way to the bar hoping the same bartender was working. They pushed and shoved their way past various stages of drunk men. Fiona turned a blind eye to the one guy who took a chance with his life after rubbing his hand on her ass. She wasn't here to start a brawl, all she wanted was information. Fiona didn't have time to explain to a drunk there was no chance in hell he would get anywhere with her. She was here for one reason. Answers.

When she reached the bar it took a while before the bartender made his way over to her. "What'll ya have?" he asked, looking as if he had already had a few himself.

"I am looking for information regarding this woman." Fiona shoved the photo across the bar.

"Honey, I think you have had enough tonight. You should get a cab, not sure you should be behind the wheel," he replied shifting his weight from one foot to the other. "Hey fellas check it out, Zayna is finally as drunk as the rest of you. She wants info on this woman." He held up the photo and showed it to the men sitting at the bar. All the men seated at the bar erupted in laughter.

One yelled, "I can tell you what position is her favorite." The entire bar exploded with laughter making it so loud it felt as if the walls were shaking.

"I assure you sir, I am completely sober, you however should think about serving breath mints at the bar instead of stale pretzels," she snatched the photo from his hand and shoved her way back to the door. She had lost Audrey in the crowd somewhere.

Fiona bent over, hands on her knees and took in a couple long deep breaths. The smell inside the bar was putrid. A mixed blend of body odor, cigar smoke and stale beer. The board of health would have a field day in there. As she straightened herself, she noticed the man who grabbed her ass when she walked in. He was alone, leaning against the building smoking a cigarette. She put the photo in her pocket, ran her fingers through her hair and slowly walked over to him. She saw him watching her out of the corner of his eye.

"What is a handsome man like you doing out here all alone?" Fiona asked doing her best to flirt even though she was repulsed by the thought.

"Listen, I don't want any trouble okay? I didn't know it was you when I touched your ass okay. The place was crowded. It was an accident. It won't happen again. I promise." The man was stammering his words. He was nervous, no longer feeling the effects of the alcohol he consumed.

"We are cool. No harm no foul. I just want to talk to you." Fiona said leaning up against the wall beside him. She was trying to act friendly and figured standing on the side of him was less confrontational than standing in front of him.

"What's on your mind these days?" he asked taking a long draw from his cigarette.

"I need some information, thought someone like you would know everything that goes on in this place." Fiona slightly turned so her body was facing him, her jacket unzipped past her chest. She could think of no better time than to use the assets God gave her.

"I don't come here that often but what is it you want to know?" he asked, this time looking at her chest instead of the ground. She had gotten his attention.

"I am looking for my sister. I heard she used to come in here all the time. Had a friend by the name Burbank. Any idea where I can find her?" Fiona asked watching the man toss his cigarette into the street.

"Zee is your sister? Man, she is a wild one. She hasn't been here lately. After what happened to Walter she just disappeared. Sorry I can't be of more help. Want to go inside, I'd like to buy you a drink and get to know you better," he asked.

"Sure, I just need to make a phone call. Why don't you go ahead inside and find us a couple seats. I will be right in." Fiona said holding her phone to her ear pretending she was calling someone.

The man opened the door to the bar and stepped aside to let people out. Audrey was the last of the group to make their way outside.

"Man, that place is a meat market. Remind me to visit here the next time I feel like shit." Audrey said with a disgusted face.

"No one in there has seen Zayna recently. The only thing I was able to get was a need for a penicillin shot." Audrey replied hoping Fiona had more to report.

"As long as you kept your tongue in your mouth Tavares I think you just need to burn the clothes you are wearing. Might be the only way to get the stench out." Fiona said walking past her towards their car.

"You're gross. May I remind you my ex-husband is a surgeon. My standards are higher than all their I.Q's put together and multiplied by ten." Audrey said pointing to the bar as she opened the car door. Fiona laughed, trying to make light of the situation when all she wanted to do was cry. She was frustrated. She needed to find Zayna and she wasn't having any luck.

"What now?" Audrey asked, after they had driven in complete silence for ten minutes.

"We are going back to the station. Find out if the boys were able to find anything and do a check on the Jeep. It shouldn't be too hard to find an army green jeep with Alaska plates. I am going to talk to Julian. He should still be in holding. Maybe he has remembered something that will help us find Zayna." Fiona stated pressing her foot on the gas pedal. She was pissed and wanted answers. Julian was the only person who was in contact with Zayana. There was more to his relationship with her and it was time he started filling in the blanks.

Fiona zipped up her jacket. The holding area was chilly. Julian was waiting in the interrogation room for her. He wasn't alone, he was sitting next to his lawyer.

"So after all your involvement you are going to hide behind Daddy's lawyer?" Fiona asked pulling out the chair, spinning it around and sitting on it backwards.

"I have told you all I know, I have nothing more to say," Julian quipped, there was a tone associated with his eyeroll.

"Oh but you haven't told me everything Julian, you and I both know that. Out of respect for you, I haven't told the task force about your part in all of this. I wanted to spare you any further humiliation. I am not sure what it was like for you down in Florida but up here we don't handle rats on our police force very well. Dirty cops have it tough enough but add rat to that list of qualifications and anything could happen between here and prison." Fiona said rocking back in her chair.

"Are you threatening my client Detective?" Julian's lawyer asked.

"No, I wouldn't say threaten. I would call it more along the lines of advice for self-preservation. Right now, I have you listed as a confidential informant. Until formal charges are filed against you in court your identity can remain a secret, but as you know I don't keep my desk as neat and tidy as you did. Anyone could walk by, see the file laying open with your name written on it, being detectives, it wouldn't take long for one of them to figure out who's who in all this. Isn't that right gentlemen?" Fiona was enjoying watching Julian quiver.

"What do you want?" the lawyer finally asked.

"I want an address, you must know where she is staying Julian. She wouldn't just contact you on the phone. There had to be some physical contact between the two of you. We dumped your phone. We know she is using a burner phone and have no way to trace it. Come on Julian, confession is good for the soul. Now is the time to pretend you have one." Fiona was getting aggressive. She wanted to reach over the table and slam his head into it but knew that wouldn't get her anywhere.

"If we don't find her, you are going down for each one of these murders alone. We have enough to charge you with Felony Murder with or without Zayna. With my help, your fancy lawyer here and your father's status, you could get the charges reduced, but not without Zayna. You have fifteen minutes, after that your name goes public along with your father's dirty little secret. I wonder how the headline will read in tomorrow morning's edition." Fiona said tucking her chair under the table. She was done here. It was now up to him.

Fiona banged on the door, letting the guard outside know they were done in here.

"Wait!" Julain screamed.

Fiona turned back to face the table. "I'm listening," was all she said.

"She left. After she attacked me she said she had one more thing to do and was booked on a boat back to Alaska. Said she needed to pick up a few things and was leaving. Once she was safely back home, she was going to send me information on where I could find the flash drive containing the video." Julian looked over at his lawyer who nodded for him to continue.

"Zayana said she wanted you to pay for taking her mother away. If it weren't for you, she would have had her mother in her life. She said something about her mother finding her years ago, they started writing letters and then one day the letters just stopped. She said you must have found out and made your mother promise never to have contact with her again." Julain looked at Fiona with somber eyes. "I am sorry Fiona, I didn't know what to do. You know I never thought it would go this far. You have got to believe me," Julian said.

"We are done here." Fiona turned and banged on the door. The guard opened the door and without turning back she walked out. She had no use for Julian anymore. She knew the only person who could stop Zayna was her. It was time to end this and Fiona knew what she needed to do.

Thirty-Nine

"I just spoke with Sergeant Morris in holding. Seems our little friend made bail. Anything you want me to do?" Audrey said into the phone.

"Keep a unit on the house. Based on his charges even daddy's influence won't keep him from being under house arrest. Put me on speaker phone." Fiona asked.

"Daniels, what have you found out?" Fiona asked hearing the rustle of papers on the other end knowing she was on speaker phone in the conference room.

"Your informant was right. The jeep is on a boat as we speak, I sent the photo to the harbor master, letting them know she isn't to get off the boat when it docks in Anchorage. There really isn't any reason for you to go Fiona. The authorities are going to arrest her as soon as the boat docks. We can have extradition paperwork sent over before she is even in custody." Detective Daniels tried to reason with her. He was beginning to have a soft spot for her.

"I am not taking any chances. She killed these women because of me and I am the one she really wants. I am the only one who can stop her. If it's a family reunion she wants then damn it that is what she is going to get." Fiona stated matter of factly. She wasn't going to let anyone dissuade her from taking down her sister. She knew it was dangerous but it's the only way. Her sister was a killer and she needed to pay. She was coming back with Zayna in handcuffs or a body bag. The choice was up to Zayna. Fiona was fine with either.

"I am going to be fine. My flight lands a few hours before the boat docks. I will be there when they arrest her, until then I am going to pay a visit to her parents and the hospital she was released from," Fiona said.

"Stay in touch with us. If you need anything make sure you let us know." Dubious said sounding like he honestly meant it.

"Thanks for all your help on this guys. I couldn't have done it without you."

" Audrey, I spoke to the Captain. If you are game, he's on board with you and I partnering up when this is all finished," Fiona said. She knew Audrey would be ecstatic. They both enjoyed working with one another.

"Sounds good to me." Audrey shouted into the phone.

"Go get our girl Mitchell. We will be waiting for you when you get back here." Daniels said into the phone.

Fiona disconnected the call and took a deep breath. The valet approached the driver's side window.

"Any luggage ma'am?" he asked. "Just a carry on. I can handle it." Fiona said.

"I will be back in three days, no need to park in the long term lot," Fiona instructed handing the valet a five dollar bill. The terminal wasn't very busy, Fiona made her way through security without any major problems. She needed to speak with the head of security regarding bringing her weapon onboard a commercial flight which was standard procedure these days. Her flight was scheduled to leave on time and she couldn't have been more excited. She was confident she was going to take her sister down. She had to. How else could she keep her mother safe?

She missed her mother, she hadn't been to see her in days. It felt as if so much had happened yet she wasn't sure her mother even realized it. There were so many questions she wanted her mother to explain but she knew a conversation like that may never happen. Perhaps it was a blessing in disguise that her mother didn't really know what was going on.

Fiona adjusted her seat for the third time, the toddler sitting behind her kept kicking the back of her chair. She was trying her best to get some sleep.

She had so much on her mind but now that she was on the plane there was nothing more she could do. Until her flight landed all she could do was think. Her brain hurt. It felt as if every muscle in her body ached. She had been sitting for three hours straight. This had been the longest she had sat down since Felicity Osborne's body was found washed up on the beach less than a week ago.

Had it really only been a week? Fiona was drained. She needed a vacation when this was all over. A long weekend some place warm. Tropical, with drinks poured into a coconut shell with an umbrella sticking out of it. The idea of a cocktail, warm sand and sun lulled Fiona to sleep.

Fiona was awoken by a stewardess tapping her on the arm.

"Ma'am. Ma'am." Fiona opened her eyes. "The captain has put the seat belt sign on. We will be landing in a few minutes. Please put on your seat belt," she said a little irritated.

Fiona glanced at her watch. She has been asleep for hours. Normally planes weren't on the top of her list of ways to travel, the idea of being suspended in midair was never a relaxing thought but she was thrilled she was at least able to get some rest. Until now, she didn't realize how exhausted she was. She had been running on empty for days.

Forty

Fiona pulled up to the house at the end of the dead end street. She double checked the address she had written down and compared it to the GPS in her rental car. The Anchorage police department didn't have any extra vehicles to lend her so she was forced to rent her own. The Captain was a very nice man but wasn't thrilled with the idea of someone outside their jurisdiction coming in and taking over. The officers in Alaska were very territorial. She didn't want to step on anyone's toes, she only wanted to introduce herself and offer her thanks for their help in apprehending one of their own residents.

Fiona looked around the neighborhood. This was a far cry from the city life she was used to. It was quiet, eerily quiet. There were very few cars on the road. She searched her GPS for a local coffee shop and couldn't find one. She wondered how these people survived without a coffee shop on every block. She looked around and realized how foreign this place seemed to her. She thought back to when she was a little girl, her and her mom always loved watching the Wizard of Oz together whenever it aired on television. "I guess I'm not in Kansas anymore," she thought to herself. She remembered how she begged her mom to buy her the VHS tape.

"What makes this movie so special is you don't see it all the time, that's why you get so excited when it comes on T.V. If you could see it everyday you would get sick of it and it won't hold the same meaning as it does now."

Smiling she knew her mother was right. When she was older she bought herself the DVD. She would put it on anytime she missed her mother once she was in the nursing home. The movie didn't have the same spark it had when she was younger. She longed to return to the days when her mother was healthy. They always had so much fun together. Fiona missed those times.

"Who is it?" the woman on the other side of the door inquired.

"Detective Mitchell Ma'am. I have some questions I'd like to ask you," Fiona stated to the wooden door. Mrs. Morgan opened the door and took a look at Fiona. Instant fear shone on her face. She tried to shut the door but Fiona used her boot to block its closure. "Mrs. Morgan, listen to me, I am Detective Fiona Mitchell. I am Zayna Morgan's sister. Please open the door, I came here talk to you about your daughter." Fiona pleaded with the woman who was using all her weight to wedge the door closed.

"Zayna is no longer my daughter. She didn't have a sister." The woman said out of breath from using all her might to try to shut the door. Fiona wasn't sure how such a tiny woman had such strength.

"Ma'am, I assure you I am a detective. Here, take a look at my shield and my police identification. I promise I am not here to hurt you. I am only looking for information regarding Zayna Morgan. May I come in? Please?" Fiona asked.

The woman, feeling more at ease now that she had seen this police woman's badge and picture I.D. opened the door extending her arm for Fiona to walk past the doorway exhaling the deep breath she had been holding.

Mrs. Morgan poured two cups of coffee from the steaming pot. "Sugar?" she asked.

"No thank you just cream if you have it," Fiona replied.

"What is it you wanted to talk to me about?" Mrs. Morgan inquired.

"I would like you to tell me about Zayna. I have only learned of her existence a few days ago. I grew up never knowing I had a twin. I don't know anything about her. Why did you adopt her?" Fiona stated stirring the cream into her coffee.

"My husband and I tried for years to have children but it just wasn't meant to be. I had several miscarriages, each one worse than the previous. It was devastating. I wanted a family so badly. Everyone I knew was having children and there I was one heartbreak after another. We decided to look into adoption. We were concerned that we were too old to adopt an infant. My husband and I were both in our mid forties at that time and didn't want to get our heart set on a baby, but one day we got the call that an infant who was just about a year old was in need of a home. Richard and I were so happy. We were finally able to have our own little family." Mrs. Morgan sat telling her story with joy in her voice.

"Did you know anything about the birth mother?" Fiona asked.

"All we were told was the child's mother was very young and placed her for adoption. The social worker explained the baby was born with severe complications and had beaten the odds. My husband and I instantly thought this baby had been waiting for us. She was a miracle. The doctors didn't think she was going to survive but she did. We adopted her and she became our own little miracle. Little did we know it wouldn't turn out as we had hoped." Mrs. Morgan now had tears in her eyes.

"What do you mean, it didn't turn out as you had hoped?" Fiona asked blowing on the hot cup of coffee thankful to finally have some caffeine flowing through her bloodstream.

"When we first brought her home, she was a delightful little baby. She laughed and spent hours laying in her crib with her feet in the air making all kinds of noise. Gibberish really, but I was convinced she knew what she was telling her feet."

"After a few years we started to notice some odd behavior. Richard was convinced there was something wrong with her. Zayna was fascinated with anything bloody. She loved to watch horror movies, when she would scrape her knee she would love to sit there and watch it bleed. She would get so angry when I would put a band aid on her boo boo. I thought she would grow up to become a doctor."

"Shortly after we adopted her my husband got transferred up here to Alaska. As I am sure you noticed there isn't much activity all the way out here. I was concerned Zayna would have trouble making friends but when she started school things seemed to get easier for her. She had made some friends but was never really close with any one girl. We had an incident in third grade, one of the children fell down the stairs and broke their collar bone. Some of the students claimed Zayna pushed her down the stairs, saying it wasn't an accident. My husband and I were outraged. Zayna was a wonderful child, she would never hurt anyone. Naturally, even though the principal couldn't prove she had anything to do with it she didn't have many friends after what happened to that little girl. She became very quiet and moody. She would have these terrible fits, throw herself on the floor and scream holy heck. It was scary to watch. My husband couldn't handle it. He started drinking just to cope with her."

"Sadly things only got worse, she would get angry and come at me with a knife. One time she actually cut me, I needed to have eleven stitches in my hand. By that point my husband had had enough. We called social services and gave her back. It was the hardest thing I ever had to do. All I ever wanted was a family but my husband was right. He knew there would come a day when she would be big enough to overpower me. Richard was petrified that he would come home from work one night and see me dead on the kitchen floor." Mrs. Morgan grabbed the napkin that was under her coffee cup and blew her nose. She felt the tears sliding down her face.

"I know you must hate me for what I did to your sister. We just didn't have any other choice. We sent her to see a therapist but nothing seemed to help. She was an angry child, nothing we did ever seemed to be enough for her." Mrs. Morgan was trying to explain.

"Please, Mrs. Morgan there is no need to explain. You did what you felt was right. I can't say I would have done anything different if I were in your shoes." Fiona tried to ease her pain.

"I loved that child, in some way I still do. She was my baby and I just gave her away. I used to hold her at night, rocking her to sleep and wonder what kind of woman would be able to give away such a precious little angel. Those thoughts came back to bite me in the ass didn't they?" Mrs. Morgan cried.

"There is no need to explain your actions Mrs. Morgan. Zayna was dangerous then. Even more so now." Fiona patted the woman's hand.

"What do you mean?" Mrs. Morgan asked looking up at Fiona. "Last I heard she was in the asylum, something about attacking her foster mother." I never tried to contact her or even her social worker but it was in the papers. It was all anyone could talk about for months after it happened. I just assumed she couldn't hurt anyone else if she were locked up there."

"So you haven't seen or heard from her?" Fiona asked.

"No, I haven't seen her at all. Richard and I moved here eight years ago. The house we used to have was far too large for us anymore. We are getting close to our eighties, there was no need to have all that room. We sold it and moved here. I don't even think she knew we moved. I can only imagine what you must think of me. Abandoning your own sister. I promise you my husband and I tried everything but in the end it just didn't work." Mrs. Morgan couldn't help but feel like she was being judged. All those years she wanted a child and after she got one and it proved to be too hard, she returned her like a defective toaster.

"Mrs. Morgan, I know you must have done everything you could."

"When my husband died a few years ago I wanted to reach out to her, let her know her father had passed but it seemed to late too reach out to her. I wouldn't even know where to find her."

"Mrs. Morgan you need to know that I didn't just come here as her sister. As I mentioned when I knocked on the door, I am also a detective. Zayna is responsible for the murder of three women and the attempted murder of another. I have reason to believe that she has returned to Alaska. If you hear from her please call me." Fiona requested placing her business card on the table next to the sugar bowl.

"Murder? Are you certain it was her?" Mrs. Morgan asked.

"Unfortunately, I am. While investigating the murders I discovered she was my sister. Until last week I never knew I had a sibling." Fiona explained. "My mother was very young when she gave birth to us. She never told me I was a twin. She suffers from Alzheimer's so at this point I am not even sure she remembers having another child. It wasn't until evidence was discovered at the crime scene and her accomplice came forward did I realize any of this." Now it was Fiona's turn to explain.

"I must warn you, Zayna is very dangerous. It wouldn't be wise to talk with her. If she contacts you please call me." Fiona repeated her request again.

Mrs. Morgan walked her to the door. "Should I be nervous Fiona, do you think she will come after me?" Mrs. Morgan looked worried.

"I don't know. If she hasn't tried to contact you yet I doubt she will now. I am going to talk to the police and have them put a unit in your neighborhood just in case," Fiona stated.

"Oh, Captain Hopkin's mother and I go to bingo together every Saturday night. He's such a kind man. When you talk to him you let him know Ida Morgan sends her regards." Mrs. Morgan stated feeling at ease knowing the police would be in the area if there were any type of emergency.

Fiona turned around to face Mrs. Morgan. "Did you say your name was Ida?" Fiona asked.

"Yes dear, Mrs. Ida Morgan," she stated. "Well Ida, it was nice talking to you. Make sure you lock this door, call me if you hear from Zayna." Fiona instructed.

Fiona turned the heat on in the car full blast. Alaska temperatures were far colder than anything she was used to. The dashboard read six degrees. Fiona blew her warm breath into her hands. Her entire body was cold and not just because of the weather. Ida. There was one more woman on Zayna's list to complete Fiona's name.

Could this be the "I" Audrey told her about? "One more thing she had to do?" Killing her adopted mother would make sense. All the other victims had something to do with adoption. It was only fitting that Zayna wanted to punish anyone who was affiliated with adoption. She took out her phone and called the police station. She wanted to make sure Mrs. Morgan was being looked after. Ida Morgan doesn't deserve to die, there had been enough suffering in that poor woman's life.

Forty-One

Fiona sat in her rental car wondering what she was going to find out when she walked through these doors. She kept the car running so she could have the heat on. The temperature rose to a balmy eleven degrees. According to the local radio station, this was a record high for this time of year. She couldn't understand who would choose to live here. A weeklong vacation maybe, but to live here full time would be more than she could handle. She was used to the four seasons, loved them all, especially summer. She loved laying on the beach, her toes in the hot sand. She tanned beautifully with little effort. She couldn't understand how anyone could live without summer.

She wasn't sure she wanted to go inside the hospital. She knew she was going to hear things that were disturbing to her. She reminded herself she was here to catch a killer, regardless of her relation to them. She needed to mentally prepare for this meeting with Zayna's doctor.

Dr. Benjamin Hastings was polite on the phone when they spoke earlier this morning. He wanted to help in any way that he could but reminded her there was a doctor patient confidentiality still in place, even though she was no longer a patient there. Fiona was going to do her best to convince the good doctor to tell her what she needed to know.

"Good Morning, how may I help you?" a blonde woman sitting behind a reception desk asked.

"I have an appointment with Dr. Hastings at eleven thirty. The name is Mitchell. Fiona Mitchell. He is expecting me." Fiona informed the woman rubbing her hands together. The building didn't seem much warmer in comparison to the frigid temperature outside.

"You aren't from around here are you honey?" she asked.
"Is it that obvious?" Fiona replied.

"Most people walk around wearing shorts in weather like this. Once you have been here for a year or two, you get acclimated to the weather. It turns your blood cold," she explained.

"Thanks, but no thanks. I don't plan on staying that long. It's far too cold for me to contemplate relocating here." Fiona smirked. She knew she was being rude but at this point she didn't care. She was mentally exhausted and wanted to put an end to this whole nightmare.

The phone rang and no sooner did the woman pick up the receiver she hung up. "The doctor will see you now. Second door on the left." Fiona nodded and proceeded down the hall. This was nothing like what she had envisioned. She thought she was going to hear patients banging on walls and yelling. She thought back to the scene in The Silence of the Lambs. This was completely different. It resembled a normal doctor's office. The halls were decorated with basic paintings of trees and old farm houses hung in weathered old frames against the stark white walls.

Fiona gently tapped on the door and waited for someone to tell her to come in. The door opened slowly. "You must be Detective Mitchell?"

"I am, and you must be Dr. Hastings?" Fiona asked not in the mood for small talk.

"The one and only," he replied with a toothy smile. She instantly thought about Julian. She wondered what he must be doing cooped up in his father's mansion under house arrest. She wasn't sure what made her think of him at this exact moment. "What can I do for you today?" Dr. Hastings said as he sat in his high back leather office chair. "Please, have a seat," he said folding his hands together on top of the table.

"As you know, a former patient of yours is wanted for a triple murder and the attempted murder of another woman. Anything you can tell me about Zayna Morgan will be helpful." Fiona stated her desire for information bluntly.

"I took over for Dr. Rego a few years before Zayna was released, so I am not sure I will be able to discuss anything she and Dr. Rego spoke about. I have spoken with our lawyers and since she hasn't been a patient with us for several years and is, as you say, a wanted fugitive, I can talk about the time I spent with her, to a degree." Dr. Hastings wanted to make sure his ass was covered. The last thing he needed was a HIPPA violation.

"It's obvious that you knew I was her twin. You didn't even flinch when you opened the door. I know I mentioned that when we spoke on the phone but I was expecting a slightly different reaction," Fiona stated.

"I have always known Zayna was a twin. It was in her file when I took over for Dr. Rego." Dr Hastings explained opening the file in front of him.

"How did you know she was a twin? I didn't even know until two days ago when DNA results from two different crimes scenes came back as an exact match for me. Thankfully her accomplice has a conscience or I would be sitting in a jail cell being charged with these murders." Fiona was shocked and didn't even try to hide her reaction.

"Please understand it has been more than ten years since I have seen Zayna Morgan. Though you do resemble her I am not sure I would have recognized either of you. She was just about twenty-one when she was released. People can change in ten plus years." Dr. Hastings explained apologetically.

"She knew she had a twin all along? Do you know how she found out? I spoke with her adoptive mother this morning and even she didn't know she was a twin. She was terrified when she opened the door and thought she was looking at Zayna."

"According to her file, her birth mother searched for her using a private detective. Once she was located here your mother sent her a letter explaining what happened when she was born." Dr. Hastings flipped the pages in the file. "Here, I have a copy of the first letter she wrote to Zayna." Dr. Hastings leaned across the desk and handed the sheet of paper to Fiona.

"First letter? So, there were others?" Fiona asked looking down at her mother's handwriting.

Dear Zayna,

I know this letter must come as a shock to you. After all these years a day has not passed that I haven't thought about my sweet little angel. When you were born, I was still a child myself. I gave birth to you and your sister before I was old enough to vote. I was terrified that I wouldn't be able to take care of you the way you would need. The doctors weren't hopeful that you would live. I did the only thing I thought was right. I gave them permission to turn off the machines. I wanted you to have the chance to experience life on your own. As I sat in the wheelchair in front of your incubator I was overcome with grief and guilt. I couldn't bear to watch you die. I was a coward then as I am now. I should have gotten on a plane to come visit you. I should be telling you this in person. You deserve at least that much but I couldn't bear the idea of you turning me away, the same way I did you.

When I was leaving the N.I.C.U I heard the faintest cry of a baby. I knew it was you. I knew you were a survivor. Deep down inside I knew you would grow up healthy and strong. I should have turned around and stayed with you. I should have brought you home and raised you the best I could. I made the biggest mistake of my life leaving you. I won't ask for forgiveness, it's not something I deserve. I want you to know that I have always loved you.

A few years ago, I contacted the agency the hospital used for adoption. They assured me you were given to a wonderful couple who would raise you with the best of everything. I was relieved that you were with a good family, in a safe and loving home. I wanted so badly to contact you but you were still so young. I didn't know if you would have been able to understand how painful it was to give you up.

I hired a private investigator to locate you once you became a teenager. I thought perhaps you were old enough to be able to understand the truth. The only thing he could find out was that you were here, in this hospital. His report said you had been in trouble with the law but couldn't gather any further details. I feel responsible for what has happened to you. If I had just taken you home perhaps things could have been different for you. I don't doubt that your parents loved you, I know I always have, I just wish I had been strong enough to fight my fears and raise you right along with your sister.

I understand if you don't want to respond to this letter. I am not sure I would if I were in your shoes. I hope that one day you can understand I never wanted anything but the best for you. I will always be here if and when you want to get to know me and your sister.

See you later Alligator,

Sincerely,

Bethany Mitchell - your mother.

Fiona wiped the tears from her eyes. Her mother knew Zayna was alive and never told her. How could she keep such a secret from me? She thought to herself. "Are there any other letters?" Fiona asked.

"There were several letters. They corresponded for years. In fact, during that time Zayna was starting to get better. I saw a major improvement after she learned about her birth mother." Dr. Hastings explained.

"I know the courts placed her here because of an incident with her foster mother but in your opinion, what was wrong with her?" Fiona asked.

"According to Dr. Rego's initial findings Zayna suffers from Reactive Attachment Disorder. When a child has been neglected at a young age, they have difficulty showing affection. They are more aggressive than loving and don't want to be comforted. Your sister spent almost an entire year in the hospital. She never had the opportunity to bond with her mother. I highly doubt she was held very often. When a child is born, new mothers are encouraged to hold their babies against their skin. It helps to create a bond between mother and child. Research has shown skin to skin contact helps the infant with optimal brain development and helps facilitate attachment. Your sister never received such care." Dr. Hastings explained this theory hoping Fiona was able to understand. He didn't want to get too detailed with medical terminology.

"Audrey was right. She and I are examples of nature versus nurture." Fiona mumbled.

"I worked with Zayna in preparation for her release into the world. I helped her get her GED and find a half-way house to live in. She and I weren't so much a physiologist and patient. I was more of a mentor to help her transition back into society. I helped her with tools to ease her anxiety. She had been here since she was a child, I petitioned the court for her release stating with continued outpatient therapy she was no longer a risk to herself or those around her. It took some convincing, the court wanted to transfer her to an adult institution but I was able to reason with them. She aged out at the age of twenty-one."

"Before her release she had a setback, which is normal for someone suffering from Reactive Attachment Disorder. Your mother stopped writing to Zayna rather abruptly. It was disturbing for her. She told me that her mother and her shared things in their correspondence with each other. When your mother stopped writing back Zayna felt abandoned all over again. Because of her disorder it was even harder for her to overcome." Dr. Hastings explained.

"If she had a set back why did you let her go?" Fiona asked accusingly.

"Detective Mitchell, this isn't a prison. We don't keep people locked up here. We treat people in the hopes they will get better and be an asset to society." Dr. Hasting's tone was getting stern.

"I understand that, but what you need to understand is I have three dead bodies and one deaf woman who will never forget what Zayna did to her. If you had done your job perhaps these murders could have been avoided." Fiona snapped back. She was tired and frustrated. Her phone chimed just as she was about to really unleash her opinion of Dr. Hastings.

"You need to call me A.S.A.P." was all the text read.

Before Fiona even had a chance to dial the phone Audrey was calling.

"What's going on?" Fiona asked unsure of the urgency.

"Where are you?"

"I am speaking with Dr. Hastings at the moment. Waiting on a call from Captain Hopkins confirming Zayna is in custody. What's wrong? You sound weird. Did something happen to my mother?" Fiona could feel the panic rise up from her feet.

"I don't know how to tell you this Fiona, but your mother is gone. We just received word from the nurse who was taking care of your mother. She went on her lunch break and when she returned to your mother's room she wasn't there. Security asked the officer if she had seen your mother. He said there was an argument in front of the nurse's station that was about to turn violent so he walked over to diffuse the situation. By the time he returned to your mother's room Marjorie was in there but your mother was gone. Security checked the tapes but they haven't been able to make a positive I.D. on the woman who was with your mother. All they could tell by the security footage is they were seen leaving the parking garage in a black SUV. Fiona I am so sorry, we are doing everything we can to find her. Dubois and Daniels are using traffic cams to see if they can get a lead on where they may be going." Audrey's voice sounded frantic.

Fiona felt helpless. The one person she wanted to protect, needed to keep safe was now missing. If Zayna was on a boat back to Alaska who could have taken her mother?

"Is everything, all right?" Dr. Hastings walked up behind her, concerned. He noticed the look of panic on Fiona's face which was concerning to him. "Hey are you alright? Here sit down." Dr. Hastings pulled a chair from against the wall to the middle of the corridor.

"My mother has been kidnapped. Someone has taken her from the nursing home. My mother is gone." Fiona mumbled. She looked like she was in shock. She was white as a ghost. Beads of perspiration were forming on her upper lip, as she started to shake.

"Fiona the best thing you can do right now is try to remain calm. Do you feel faint? Put your head between your knees if you need to. I am going to get you some water. I will be right back." Dr. Hastings walked towards the reception area.

Fiona took a deep breath and held it in. She mentally counted to ten and then slowly exhaled. She told herself to feel her feet on the floor. "Feel your butt sitting in the chair. Relax your body and feel yourself in the chair. You are fine. Everything is going to be fine. Just take a moment and breathe, in and out." she told herself. Fiona knew a panic attack was imminent. She used to suffer from them when she was a teenager. The kids in school would bully her and it would cause her to freak out. Her mother taught her the breathing technique which helped more than she realized. It had been years since she experienced this feeling, even after Arthur she was too grief stricken to have a panic attack. She needed her mother. Her mother had a way about her, always able to make Fiona feel safe and secure.

Fiona's cell phone rang. She reached inside her pocket for her phone but her pocket was empty. She heard the continuous ring and finally realized her phone had been in her hand the entire time. She needed to pull herself together. She was no good to her mother if she were to fall apart.

"Mitchell!" she screamed into the phone.

"Detective Mitchell, this is Captain Hopkins. I wanted to let you know we have a woman in custody. I am not sure she is the one you were waiting on. She doesn't look anything like you. She had red hair but that's about all that is a match for you."

"What do you mean you have a woman. Is it Zayna Morgan or not?" Fiona was furious.

"We are running her prints now but I don't think she is your sister. She claims she came to Alaska to meet some friends from college. She bought the Jeep from a man before she left. She was going to be here for a few weeks and didn't want to rent a car. She was going to leave the Jeep with her friends when she returned home. I honestly don't think she is your sister. So far her story checks out. She is scared shitless." The captain explained knowing this was not the news Fiona was hoping for.

"Show her the photo of Zayna and find out if she recognizes her. She said she bought the car from a man? I am going to send you a photo of Julian Corriera let me know if she recognizes his face." Fiona heard her phone chime, she was getting another call.

"Mitchell!" she screamed into the phone. She needed to calm down. She could feel herself coming unglued. As panicked as she was about her mother's disappearance, she was thousands of miles away. She couldn't do a damn thing from Alaska. She trusted Audrey would stop at nothing to find her. Right now, she needed to find out who this woman was the Alaska police has in custody and what her involvement was in all of this.

"Detective Mitchell, this is Ida Morgan. I need your help. I went to the market this morning to get a couple things to make for dinner. I know it sounds crazy but I think someone was following me." Mrs. Morgan shared a similar sound of panic in her voice as Fiona.

"Are you home now?"

"Yes, I just got home. I think a car followed me home but I am looking out the window and I don't see it anymore." She explained.

"Do you know what kind of car it was?" Fiona asked.

"Oh dear, I am almost eighty. My eyesight isn't what it used to be. It was dark blue or black. I am not sure. It was one of those big cars, the kind you see drug dealers drive on those criminal T.V. shows."

"Like an Escalade? Big wheels, high off the ground?" Fiona was trying to get as much of a description as she could so she could have a local officer patrol the area.

"I think so. I am sorry, I shouldn't have called. I have been on edge since you told me about Zayna. I didn't mean to bother you." Mrs. Morgan sounded embarrassed.

"You aren't bothering me. I want you to lock all the doors and stay in the house. If anything happens call 9-1-1. I will come by in about an hour. I have something I need to finish up and then I will swing by. Please Ida, make sure you lock all your doors." Fiona instructed.

"Here's some water. How are you doing?" Dr. Hastings asked worried she was going to pass out.

"I am feeling a little better, all things considered. I have detectives back home looking for my mother. I need to get to the station. There seems to be some confusion as to who was actually on the boat. Looks like Zayna may have slipped through my fingers again." Fiona drained the water bottle and crumpled the empty plastic bottle with her hand. She was furious but knew she needed to stay in control.

"I am going with you. I know Zayna. I know how to read her. If the woman on the boat knows more than they are saying, I may be able to help." Dr. Hastings pushed his office door open and leaned in to grab his coat.

"Dr. Hastings, your mother is asking for you. What shall I tell her?" the receptionist inquired.

"Tell her to consult her own doctor. She is my mother, not my patient." He snapped back looking irritated.

"Your mother is a patient here?" Fiona asked with a raised eyebrow.

"It's a long story."

"We have a fifty-mile drive to the police station; I think we have time. It will take my mind off all of this for a bit." Fiona shot him a smile she knew he wouldn't be able to resist.

Forty-Two

The heat in the car felt soothing to Fiona. She adjusted the passenger seat to get comfortable and switched the seat warmer to high. "Ok, let me have it Ben. Is it okay that I call you Ben?" she asked not sure how formal he was.

"Ben is fine as long as I can call you Fiona." He smiled back at her. Two could play that game. "My mother raised me on her own. I never knew who my father was the entire time I was growing up. My mother's marriage didn't last long. She married because she was pregnant with me. She said her family would disown her if she had a child out of wedlock. Her husband was long gone before I was old enough to remember him. She never led me to believe her husband was my father. She made that very clear but never told me who my biological father was. It wasn't until she starting drinking that she started to say things that didn't make sense. She said things that couldn't be possible. When she was sober I would ask her about the things she said and she would deny it, saying she was tipsy and didn't know what she was saying. At first, I believed her. She was my mother, why would she lie? It wasn't until right about the time I started college that I realized the things she was saying may be true."

"One night I decided to drive home from college and surprise my mother with a weekend visit. I didn't come home much; I had my own life. Anytime I would talk with her I could tell she had been drinking and it started to worry me. I knew I needed to check on her more often. My mother was always fun to be around. So that night I drove all the way home to surprise her. I came in the house with my laundry and heard arguing. As I went upstairs to my old room the voices were getting louder. I went to my mother's room, the door wasn't completely shut. My mother was in her bed, naked with just the bed sheet wrapped across the front of her chest. At the foot of the bed was my uncle, in his boxer shorts. You can only imagine the shock of what I was witnessing. My mother and her own brother, both pretty much naked. It wasn't hard to figure out what was happening."

"Naturally my mother was mortified that I had found out. After my uncle stormed out of the house she finally confessed the truth." Ben looked over to Fiona who was sitting in the passenger seat, her eyes as large as golf balls.

"Oh my God, your poor mother," was all Fiona could think to say.

"My poor mother? I was in shock but trust me, you haven't heard the worst of it. Once my mother got dressed she found me in my room. I was sitting on the edge of my bed holding my head in my hands. It became clear why my mother was drinking so much. She proceeded to explain that her and my uncle were in love with each other. They had been for years. No one in the family knew, they had gotten really good at keeping it a secret. From what she told me, their affair, if you want to call it that, started back when they were in their late teens and had been going on all this time. My uncle wanted to end things with my mother, he wanted to focus on his career and didn't want their relationship to conflict with his profession. She was devastated. She spent that entire weekend in bed crying, she was inconsolable. She wouldn't eat, she wouldn't get out of bed. Nothing I tried worked. She was a mess. I didn't know what to do. I tried to talk to her about it but she was too ashamed. She finally opened up a little but became hysterical all over again. She finally told me everything. After that, I had no idea how to help her. I called her physician and we decided it was best for my mother if she were admitted to an inpatient facility. She has been there ever since." Ben couldn't believe he had just told Fiona, a perfect stranger his family's dirty little secret.

"Your mother has been in the hospital all these years?" Fiona asked.

"Yes, she has never gotten over losing her brother, the love of her life as she refers to him."

"How did you handle all of this?" Fiona asked, In her opinion he seemed to be a normal well-rounded adult, but clearly everyone has skeletons in their closet.

"It was difficult. Once mom was put away, I was left all alone to deal with everything. I had to come up with a reason for why she was in the hospital. My family didn't need to know about her and my uncle. I covered it as best I could. Just before she went to the hospital, she finally told me who my real father was. Fiona, I am the product of incest. My uncle is my biological father." It was obvious Ben hadn't had much practice saying those words out loud.

"Wow, that must have been a shock. Luckily you are driving with a woman who is familiar with family secrets. If it weren't for these murders, I would never have known I had a sister. My mother never mentioned her to me. She suffers from early onset Alzheimer's. I don't even know if she remembers Zayna at this point which is why I am beside myself knowing she is missing. She could be anywhere and not have any idea she is missing." Fiona mentioned.

"Your mother has Alzheimer's? When did it start?" Ben asked.

"She started to show signs when I was still in high school but it didn't get really bad until I was in my early twenties. Having to place her in a nursing home at such a young age was the hardest decision of my life. I love my mother dearly, but I also love being a police officer. She wouldn't have wanted me to give that up in order to take care of her." Fiona felt guilty just saying the words out loud.

"This makes perfect sense. When Zayna had her set back it was right around the same time your mother stopped writing to her, that had to be about the time she started showing signs of her illness. Zayna blamed you for taking her mother away from her. She felt you were the number one daughter and she was a second-class citizen. Man, this all makes perfect sense."

"My sister is a killer, that's not my fault. I didn't know anything about her. I didn't know my mother was writing her letters. I never saw any letters in the house growing up. This is all so hard to believe. My mother wouldn't keep something like this from me. We have always been honest with each other, at least I used to think so. Now, I am not sure about anything." Fiona put her head against the passenger side window, wondering if there was more to her life that was a lie.

"There is something else that I need to tell you. Something that you aren't going to like hearing but I feel it's something you need to know even if it won't help your current situation." Ben was apprehensive, he knew Fiona would never understand what he was about to tell her. He wasn't sure anyone would.

"You don't have to say anything." Fiona lifted her head off the window and looked at him. "Whatever happened in your family is none of my business." She didn't want him to admit to something she already knew. There was no sense in humiliating him if she could avoid it.

"You don't understand, your sister was released because of me. Dr. Rego didn't think she was fit to be released and was going to recommend she be transferred to the adult facility for another five years. I couldn't let that happen. I wouldn't let that happen. I convinced Dr. Rego to turn her case over to me so that I could handle her release the way I needed to." Ben started to explain.

This part she didn't know. She didn't realize the good doctor was willing to help a dangerous criminal to get released. She had a pretty good idea what his reason was.

"Go on." She encouraged.

"Somehow Zayna found out about my family. She used it against me. She told me if I got her released, she would forget what she knew and I would never hear from her again. I used every influence I had to ensure her release. Once she left, I never heard anything about her again until yesterday when I got your phone call." Ben felt like a weight had been lifted from his shoulders. He had been carrying around his family's secret for years, never trusting anyone enough to divulge that part of his life.

"Is Governor Correira aware that you know he is your biological father?" Fiona asked not lifting her head from the window. They were less than fifteen minutes from the police station according to the GPS device on the dash board. Fiona wanted to just cut to the chase.

Ben turned to look at Fiona, for a split second he forgot he was behind the wheel and the car veered a little too close to the side barely missing the guard rail. "How did you know he is my father?" Ben was shocked Fiona had knowledge of his family tree.

"I told you earlier we had Zayna's accomplice in custody. When was the last time you spoke with your Uncle?" Fiona inquired.

"Once I became aware of my mother's real relationship with my Uncle, I severed all ties with him. I heard about him becoming Governor but I haven't had any contact with him in years. Why do you ask?" Ben questioned Fiona with intrigue in his voice.

"I didn't think I would be the one telling you this but your Uncle has another child. Julian Correira. He is a detective and was assigned to my division as my new partner. It turns out he was also being blackmailed by Zayna. He knows about your mother and his father." Fiona felt terrible, she had no intention of hurting anyone. She just wanted her sister to pay for her crimes.

"Your sister is a bitch!" Ben yelled slamming his hand on the steering wheel. "I'm sorry, that was inappropriate. I tell my patients all the time never to outsource blame that belongs in your own backyard. She wasn't involved with the relationship between my mother and uncle, but if she wanted revenge on you and your mother, she should have found a way to do it without involving innocent people." He looked over to Fiona apologetically. "I'm sorry none of this is coming out right. Damn it! I must sound like my patients and not their physician." He grumbled.

"Don't think I haven't thought the same thing about Zayna. She not only took the lives of three innocent people, in the process she ruined a man's career and holds the key to ruining the lives of your family. She is quite the bitch." Fiona was glad someone else was just as furious as she was. Zayna has left a path of innocent people in her wake just to get revenge on her and her mother, for which neither did anything wrong. Fiona told herself that she would have been open to the idea of having a sister even if she had mental health issues. Had she known anything about her she would have written and told Zayna her mom was ill and wasn't going to get any better. Why didn't her mother tell her she had a sister? Even now she still couldn't wrap her mind around the fact that her mother kept this kind of secret from her.

Forty-Three

Captain Hopkins was waiting for Fiona at the door of the police station. He was eager to put this situation to rest. He wasn't thrilled about her causing this much of a commotion within his department. The sooner she was on a plane the happier he would be.

"Captain, where is she?" Fiona demanded. She was done with the formalities; it was time for answers.

"I have her in interrogation room three. She is extremely upset. I would go easy on her. She said she doesn't know anything about your sister." The captain was concerned Fiona was going to explode once she got into the interrogation room.

"I will make that determination, Captain. Thank you for keeping her here, I know this was an inconvenience for you." Fiona hoped she sounded sincere. She really could have cared less what the captain thought at this point. He needed to stay out of her way and let her do the one thing she traveled thousands of miles to do, arrest her sister.

"You need to wait out here. I need to speak with her privately. You aren't her physician so there are no legal grounds for you to be present when I question her." Fiona was thankful Ben was with her. Their conversation during the drive over, though painful, kept her mind occupied. She hasn't been able to focus on anything other than this case for almost a week. Her brain needed the break.

"I will be right here if you need me. I find all of this fascinating. I know that isn't politically correct to say but I do. I am familiar with what happens once someone commits a crime and gets admitted to my hospital. I have never experienced this side of an investigation." Ben was embarrassed, he knew he was acting like a little boy seeing a fire truck racing down the street.

"I get it. It is interesting when you are sitting on the sidelines, normally I find my cases very intriguing but this one is making my blood boil. Zayna needs to pay for what she's done. If you would like, you can sit in that room over there. It has a two-way mirror. You can watch me interrogate her. It's as close as I can get you without breaking any laws." Fiona felt it was the least she could do. She felt awful having to tell him about his half-brother being involved in all this.

"I would love that. Thanks!" Ben was excited beyond measure. He has watched crime shows on television but had never had an opportunity to see something like this in person.

Fiona walked into the interrogation room and took a seat opposite a woman who clearly wasn't her sister. In fact, the mop of red hair on her head was the only feature they had in common.

"So the Captain has informed me you purchased the Jeep just before you got aboard the boat to come back to Alaska?" Fiona asked.

"Yes, I wanted to have my own car while I was here. My friends and I have several things planned and it's easier than renting a car."

Fiona looked down at the file sitting on the table. There were some confusing facts in the file that she needed clarification on.

"Ms. Michaels is it?" Fiona asked.

"Yes, Brenda Michaels."

"I see here in the file there is a copy of your Alaska driver's license. What I don't see is a Bill of Sale for the vehicle you purchased. We ran the plates through our database and it has been reported stolen. As of now you are under arrest for grand larceny." Fiona could instantly see Brenda's expression change. She had no idea the car was reported stolen.

Fiona heard a small knock on the mirror. She thought she could trust Ben. She told him the only way he could sit on the other side of the two-way mirror was if he promised to be quiet.

"I will be right back. I need to check on some things and then perhaps when I come back you will tell me the truth."

Fiona closed the door just as Ben opened his. "I thought I told you not to make a sound. I need to break her. I know she is lying about buying the Jeep. This could take a while. I understand if you need to get back to the hospital. I can get one of the officers to drive me back later to get my rental." Fiona didn't want to hold him up, assuming he had obligations that needed to be met.

"I know this woman." Ben said looking down at his shoes.

"What do you mean you know her?" Fiona asked.

"She was a patient at the hospital. I wasn't sure at first but when she said her name it all clicked. She was in the same therapy group as your sister. Brenda Michaels wasn't a patient for very long. If memory serves she was ordered by the court to undergo thirty day treatment for anger management. She had a tendency to get violent. From what I remember she wasn't a difficult patient, released without issues I believe."

"Well well, who knew you were going to come in handy today Ben. Why don't you come back into the room with me. Since you were once her physician you can help me question her," Fiona suggested.

"Whatever you say Boss Lady." Ben said walking behind her into the interrogation room.

Fiona cringed when she heard him refer to her as boss lady. Julian used to call her that, what an insufferable prick he turned out to be.

Brenda sat up straight when she heard the door open. It was obvious the tears hadn't stopped when Fiona had left the room.

"What is he doing here? Listen I will tell you anything you want to know but you have to promise you won't send me back there." Brenda cried.

Fiona nodded to Ben to give him the okay to speak to Brenda.

"Brenda no one is going to send you back to the hospital. I need you to cooperate with the Detective. You need to tell her exactly how you got the Jeep. I am sure the detective will put in a good word with the D.A. if you cooperate." Ben was calm when he spoke, his voice sounded different. He was Dr. Ben Hastings instead of just Ben.

"I didn't want to do it. She made me. She said if I didn't do it, she would kill me. She had a knife. I didn't know what else to do." Brenda was hysterical. The tears were streaming down her eyes, along with the last bit of her mascara.

"Who? Who made you take the Jeep?" Fiona knew her initial story was bullshit. From the moment this woman opened her mouth all that came out were lies.

"Zayna Morgan. We met in the hospital. When I was released, I worked hard at getting better. I went to college and tried to make something of myself. I don't know how she found me but she did. That woman is terrifying. I remember her from group therapy but something was different about her. Her eyes were dark, almost black, as if there was no one inside her." Brenda was finally telling the truth. Fiona needed to know everything Brenda knew, it may be the only way to find her sister, a diabolical serial killer.

"Brenda, why did she want you to take the Jeep?" Ben chimed in.

"She said her twin sister was on to her and she needed to throw her off the scent. She had work to do. Something about her mother." Brenda said wiping her nose with the back of her hand.

"Did she say what she planned to do about my mother?" Fiona asked furious at the idea of Zayna harming her mother.

"She didn't say. She was acting strange. She was nervous, in a hurry like she was late for something. She gave me the keys to the Jeep and said the ticket was in the glove box. The ticket was in her name, I was nervous I was going to get in trouble with the Harbor Master but he didn't even notice. Detective, what's going to happen to me?" Brenda stated.

That little bitch wanted me to think she was leaving town, she knew I would follow her. How stupid am I? Fiona thought to herself, trying to keep herself calm. She didn't want to take her anger out on Brenda, after all she was a victim in all this just like her.

"I will speak with the captain. Your file shows you haven't been in any trouble. You are still in school?" Fiona inquired

"Yes, this is my last year. I am scheduled to graduate in June. I had no intention of coming back here. My parents still live here but they come to visit me instead of the other way around. They think it's best that I start a new life somewhere where I am not surrounded by bad memories." Brenda took a deep breath and wiped her eyes.

"I don't see why we can't forget about this little incident. Call your parents and have them come pick you up." Fiona gave Brenda a smile, there was no reason to complicate Brenda's life any more.

"Brenda, I know this must have been extremely scary for you. While you are here if you want to talk feel free to contact me." Ben slid his business card across the steel table. Brenda put it in her pocket and gave Ben a simple nod.

"Thanks for your help in there. I really appreciate it." Fiona extended her arm to shake Ben's hand.

"No problem, I am just glad it all worked out for Brenda. She was a good kid and from what I can tell she has worked hard to put her past behind her. Thanks for cutting her a break." Ben replied.

"She seems like she has her head on her shoulders. Evidently my sister has the ability to manipulate anyone she comes in contact with. I need to get back home and find my mother, and Zayna." Fiona was talking to Ben but trying to plan her next step.

"Do you need me to drive you to the airport? I can take your rental back if you have a plane to catch." Ben offered.

"I am scheduled to leave later tonight, but thanks for the offer." Fiona smiled at Ben. He was handsome, educated and the fact that his family was as screwed up as hers created a spark between them. She wasn't in the market for a relationship but there was something endearing about him.

"Well, you need to eat. How about an early dinner before you have to leave? My treat." Ben offered his cheeks turning red.

"That sounds like a great idea. I could use a good meal. I feel like I haven't eaten real food in weeks. Thank heavens for power bars," she joked.

"Okay, it's a date." Ben said smiling.

"Shit, I forgot about Mrs. Morgan. I told her I would stop by. She has been a nervous wreck since I showed up on her doorstep this morning. She called earlier and said she thought someone was following her in the market. I need to get over there. Raincheck on dinner?" Fiona asked bummed, she wasn't going to spend more time with Ben.

"Why don't I drop you off at Mrs. Morgan's. You can explain to her that Zayna isn't in the state. Hopefully that will put her at ease. I can pick you back up in a couple hours and we can have dinner then head straight to the airport." Ben was trying to quickly think of a way to see her again before she left.

"You're a prince you know that? Let's go," Fiona said patting him on the shoulder.

Forty-Four

Fiona tried Mrs. Morgan's home number for the third time. Still there was no answer. She was relieved Zayna wasn't actually in Alaska, at least Mrs. Morgan would be safe. Fiona was still worried about her mother. Audrey's latest text mentioned they were working on a few possible leads. Audrey assured her the entire task force was working on nothing else but trying to find her mother. Even though Fiona was out of her mind with worry, she felt comforted in the fact that the task force was working diligently on Fiona's behalf. She wanted to change her reputation on the force after Arthur, in the process she made actual friends without even realizing it.

"I don't know why she isn't answering. I told her to lock all the doors and stay in the house. I doubt she would have gone anywhere." Fiona mentioned to Ben.

"Maybe she's just scared and doesn't want to answer the phone thinking Zayna may call. I am sure she is fine. Your sister is thousands of miles away. Once you tell Mrs. Morgan that she will feel much more relaxed," Ben explained.

Ben pulled up in front of the house Fiona pointed at, he put the car in park but left the engine running.

"Are you sure you don't want me to go in with you?" Ben asked for a second time.

"No, I am sure she is fine but thanks for the offer." Fiona said. She was glad to have someone on her side.

"Alright. I will text you in a couple hours and we can decide on dinner." Ben said as Fiona unbuckled her seat belt, opening the car door.

"Sounds good. Hey Ben, thanks." She gave him a smile and slammed the car door shut.

Ben waved as he drove off down the street.

Fiona knocked on the door. She rang the bell but Mrs. Morgan must not have heard it. After a couple minutes the cold was beginning to seep into her bones. She put her hands in her pocket and realized she left her phone in Ben's car. "Son of a bitch!" she yelled stomping her foot on the porch. She needed to be able to communicate with Audrey in case there were any developments in finding her mother. Once Mrs. Morgan answered the door, she would call Audrey from inside and give her Mrs. Morgan phone number so she could have some contact with her team back home until Ben came back to get her.

Fiona finally gave in, waving the proverbial white flag. The cold was simply more than she could handle. She tried the door and was glad it wasn't locked, even though she had told her to keep all her doors locked. Fiona was used to flighty women. Her mother always forgot to lock the door or turn off the lights. Fiona thought about her mother. She prayed wherever she was she wasn't scared. The idea of her mother not knowing where she was, in a strange place, with someone dangerous, daughter or not made Fiona's skin crawl.

She did her best to remain calm because there was absolutely nothing she could do until her flight later tonight. She needed to trust that Audrey was doing everything she could back home to find her mother. Fiona made her way into the house. Nothing seemed out of place since she was here earlier this morning.

"Mrs. Morgan? Anyone home?" she yelled. Fiona drew her weapon. She didn't want to startle Mrs. Morgan but if she learned nothing from an open door it was to be on alert.

Fiona turned to make sure there was no one in the living room with her. She was paranoid, the last time she was in someone's house she found Julian on the balcony freezing. As she approached the kitchen, she noticed something out of the corner of her eye. She wasn't positive as to what she saw and took one step forward. There was no mistaking what she was looking at. There, beside the kitchen chair was a pair of loafers. Brown leather loafers. As she approached the kitchen, she saw the loafers, and the feet in them that were connected to a pair of legs. Mrs. Morgan was on the floor. Fiona quickly made her way around the table and immediately fell to her knees.

"Mrs. Morgan can you hear me?" Fiona yelled to the unconscious woman laid out on the floor. Her throat had been slit, blood still seeping onto the floor. "Hang on, you are going to be alright." Fiona moved Mrs. Morgan's hand from her throat, her fingers looked like someone poured a can of red paint onto them. The smell of iron filled the room. Fiona knew there was nothing she could do for this poor woman. Even if the paramedics were already here there was no way to save her. Based on the amount of blood that was still seeping from her throat combined with the large puddle gathering on the floor, Mrs. Morgan barely had minutes left in this world.

"I am so sorry Mrs. Morgan. I am so sorry this happened to you." Fiona said with tears in her eyes. She was exhausted, both mentally and physically. She was tired of dead bodies and blood splatters, but most of all she was tired of being forced to play this game with her sister. Fiona used her left hand since it was the cleanest of the two even though there was still blood on both her hands and closed Mrs. Morgan's eyes. She was gone. Fiona sat back on the haunches of her legs and started to sob uncontrollably. She cried for Mrs. Morgan, Felicity Osborne, Amelia Leach and all the other people who were harmed by the hand of a serial killer.

Fiona heard the front door open and the back door just beyond the kitchen was kicked in. She looked up and saw various men dressed in black S.W.A.T. gear storm into the house.

"Put your hands in the air and slowly stand up!" one man yelled, holding a glock just a few yards from her head.

Fiona put her hands in the air. "I am a detective. My name is Fiona Mitchell, badge number 31541."

A large man, dressed in the same S.W.A.T. attire stood behind and grabbed her left wrist and brought it around to her back, then with the right. He frisked her roughly. She heard the click of the handcuffs.

"Officer, there has been a mistake. I am a detective. Please call Captatin Hopkins, he will corroborate what I am telling you. I was with him less than an hour ago." Fiona pleaded with the arresting officer to listen to her.

"We know all about you Zayna Morgan. Someone placed an anonymous call to 9-1-1 informing us you were here and was threatening to kill the owner of the home." The arresting officer explained to Fiona as he read off the Miranda Rights to her.

"You have got this all wrong. Zayna Morgan is my twin sister. I had nothing to do with Mrs. Morgan's death. When I got here, she was already bleeding out on the floor. Please why won't you believe me?" she cried.

"You can explain yourself down at the station. Until then, I would shut up and wait for a lawyer. I took the liberty of taking a look at your rap sheet. I am sure you are familiar with needing a lawyer." The officer was immensely cocky.

Forty-Five

"Where are we going?" Bethany asked Fiona. She sat quietly in the car; her hands folded gently in her lap.

"Mom for the hundredth time, we are going to visit a friend of mine." Zayna answered frustrated at having to answer the same question over and over.

"I think you are driving a little fast aren't you?" her mother said, placing the palm of her hand on the handle of the passenger seat door.

"Mom, just sit still until we get there. I know how to drive, I am an adult you know." Zayna was done trying to play nice. Her mother was wearing her out. Everything she did took so long now that her mother was with her. She never realized how much work it is to take care of someone who couldn't remember things that happened an hour ago. Knowing she had taken her mother from Fiona was what was keeping her from really freaking out. She knew Fiona was sitting in a jail cell in Alaska.

"Let's see her try to get out of that one." She mumbled to herself. Zayna's plan had worked. Brenda was the lynch pin to all of this and she was thrilled she held up her end of the bargain. All she needed to do now was deposit the money into Brenda's account and everything would be done. Twenty-five thousand dollars is a small price to pay to frame her sister for Mrs. Morgan's murder.

"Okay mom we're here." Zayna looked over at her mother as she unfastened her seatbelt. "You ready to meet my friends?" she asked.

"Of course, any friend of yours is a friend of mine. Are these buddies of yours from the police department, Fiona?" Bethany asked starting to get excited about this adventure they were on.

"Sure mom." Zayna said setting the alarm on the black S.U.V

They approached the walkway, the wind blowing their hair sideways.

"Your friend has a fancy home. Much fancier than our house." Bethany was in awe of the mansion set before her. I hope I look okay, I wouldn't want to embarrass you in front of your friends."

"You look fine mom, it's not that big of a deal. We are just going to pick up something. We won't stay long." Zayna replied annoyed with her mother.

"Whatever you want to do. I am just glad I get to spend some time with you. You have been so busy working on that case, I haven't seen you all that much." Bethany said rubbing Fiona's arm.

"I told you, that case is all over. Now we can spend a lot more time together." Zayna wrapped her arm around her mother's shoulder after ringing the doorbell.

"Hey girl, come on in. We were just sitting in the parlor having a midday cocktail. You know what they say, It's five o'clock somewhere." The man at the door held his rocks glass in the air as a salutation.

"Mom, I would like you to meet Julian Corriera, he and I are old friends. Julian, this is my mother Bethany." Zayna introduced them as she fixed her hair in the reflection on the glass door.

"It's a pleasure to meet you Julian. My daughter speaks very highly of you." Bethany replied, always knowing how to act in any social situation.

"It's a pleasure to meet you as well, I can see now where your daughter gets her good looks from. My parents are in the parlor. Can I interest you in a cocktail? I am sure they would love to meet you." Julian ushered the two women into the adjoining room.

"That would be lovely, wouldn't it Fiona?" Bethany looked at Fiona with a nod of approval.

"Sure thing. Let's go." Zayna followed into the parlor.

"Is there something wrong Bethany?" Julian asked concerned by the look on the woman's face.

"Who is that man standing over there?" Bethany asked suddenly feeling cold.

"That man is Governor Correira and also my father." Julian explained. He has been around people who were in awe of his father. Being Governor held a certain social status.

Bethany walked over to the Governor, her back straight arms by her side.

"Well hello Manuel. Long time no see. By the looks of things, I see you have done very well for yourself." Bethany said in a snarky tone.

"Please forgive my mother. She gets confused easily. She must think you are someone else." Zayna explained starting to get embarrassed.

"Fiona please, I am not confused. Manuel knows damn well who I am, don't you Manuel? Though you used to prefer to be called Manny but now that you are a high class Governor I can understand why you would want to come off more regal." Bethany snapped.

"Mom, what the hell are you talking about?" Zayna yelled.

"Fiona, I would like you to meet your father." Bethany said with fire in her voice.

The entire room fell silent, you could hear the ice cubes clank in the rocks glasses as they melted, no one knew what to say. Finally the silence was broken when Zayna finally opened her mouth

"Governor Manuel Correira is my father?" Zayna asked unaware there was anyone in the room other than her mother.

"Yes dear, and now it's time I tell you about your sister…

Acknowledgements

I may have written all seventy thousand plus words but I didn't get here alone. Many people took part in this adventure right along with me. There are several people that I need to thank for helping make this book possible.

Jocelyn and Charlotte Carvalho, you two hold a special place in my heart that words could never describe. I held each of you the day you were born and promised to be the best Aunt the world has ever seen. I hope that I have lived up to the title. When I first decided to write this book, I knew instantly who I would dedicate it to. You two have been a shining light in my life. I hope this book makes you proud. Let this book be a symbol that dreams do come true. May neither of you ever lose your spark.

Mrs. Colleen Brightman, thank you for the numerous texts, emails with thumbs up emojis when reading chapter by chapter as they were written. Your editing skills are greatly appreciated. Per your request, Bethany Mitchell, is still among the living throughout this entire book, though I make no promises for her livelihood in book two. When we met, I never imagined you would have joined my book club or agreed to take this book ride with me. Hopefully you are ready for book two because you and I are in this together.

Devin Flood, thank you for designing the book cover. Your talent amazes me. We have known each other for as long as I can remember and each picture you create takes my breath away. Don't ever lose sight of your talent.

For my lifelong friend, Meghan Flood. I gave you the freedom to create the name of one of the characters in the book and with that Audrey Tavares was born. I hope after reading this you can see some of yourself in Audrey, a bad ass detective with a soft heart. Thank you for everything you have done for me in the last forty years. I can't wait to see where the next forty years takes us.

I also need to thank my nephew, the one I refer to as, my first born. Geoffrey Boucher Flood, you are one of the three loves of my life. Your hard work and dedication to everything you do amazes me, especially since I am ready to give up if I don't get something right the first time. I hope you enjoy reading about Dr. Benjamin Hastings as much as I have enjoyed creating his character.

What makes this next group of people so special is I have only known them for less than five years and each one of them mean as much to me as the ones I have already mentioned. Like snowflakes, no two are alike.

My boss, Michelle Barton, thank you for keeping me gainfully employed in case this whole book thing doesn't work out. You make me laugh every day with your need for chocolate, your ability to forgive any mistakes that I may make, and most of all your patience.

My work person. The Monica to my Rachel, the Rory to my Loreali. Alicia Bedient, you keep me laughing all day long. We created an instant connection and have been in the thick of it since day one. There is no building, character or anything substantial in this book based on you, BUT some of the comments that Fiona says come straight from your mouth, my favorites being "Well you look like shit run over twice." And "Doesn't anyone have an effing vest in this house" Thank you for all the movie quotes, friends references and your funny childhood stories

Sheri Hansen, I am not sure where to begin when it comes to thanking you for all you have done. You have been by far the most excited about this entire adventure. You have had dreams not only about this book but the sequel that I hadn't given any thought to at the time. You have taught me self-love, being secure in who I am regardless of what the world may think. Nurse Hansen has a bit part in this book but she is going to appear in book two in a way that will give you goosebumps. Thank you for your encouragement, your contagious giggle and providing this starving artist with copious amounts of string cheese, salad and cauliflower fried rice.

Mr. Mark Leach, You and I have a bond like no other. Two of the most unlikely people to become friends and yet here we are. You were there on the absolute worst day of my life, the moment my life literally changed in a New York Minute and have stuck by my side every minute since then. I am honored to call you my friend. Anytime I was wanting to give up you wouldn't let me. You have always been my strongest supporter. You always know the right words to say to keep me motivated. When I felt like I wasn't going to make it through another day, another hour, or minute and needed a laugh you would text me silly movie quotes to make me smile. You are the reason this book was transformed from a "I wish I could" to a dream I can hold in my hands. If I never have a nickel, because of your friendship I will always be as rich as a Rockefeller.

Made in the USA
Monee, IL
10 October 2021